# The Kreutzer Sonata

## and Other Stories

## Count Leo Tolstoi

# Copyright Notice

# CONTENTS

# 1

# STORY 1

## THE KREUTZER SONATA

\*\*\*

# CHAPTER I

Travellers left and entered our car at every stopping of the train. Three persons, however, remained, bound, like myself, for the farthest station: a lady neither young nor pretty, smoking cigarettes, with a thin face, a cap on her head, and wearing a semi-masculine outer garment; then her companion, a very loquacious gentleman of about forty years, with baggage entirely new and arranged in an orderly manner; then a gentleman who held himself entirely aloof, short in stature, very nervous, of uncertain age, with bright eyes, not pronounced in color, but extremely attractive, – eyes that darted with rapidity from one object to another.

This gentleman, during almost all the journey thus far, had entered into conversation with no fellow-traveller, as if he carefully avoided all acquaintance. When spoken to, he answered curtly and decisively, and began to look out of the car window obstinately.

Yet it seemed to me that the solitude weighed upon him. He seemed to perceive that I understood this, and when our eyes met, as happened frequently, since we were sitting almost opposite each other, he turned away his head, and avoided conversation with me as much as with the others. At nightfall, during a stop at a large station, the gentleman with the fine baggage – a lawyer, as I have since learned – got out with his companion to drink some tea at the restaurant. During their absence several new travellers entered the car, among whom was a tall old man, shaven and wrinkled, evidently a merchant, wearing a large heavily-lined cloak and a big cap. This merchant sat down opposite the empty seats of the lawyer and his companion, and straightway entered into conversation with a young man who seemed like an employee in some commercial house, and who had likewise just boarded the train. At first the clerk had remarked that the seat opposite was occupied, and the old man had answered that he should get out at the first station. Thus their conversation started.

I was sitting not far from these two travellers, and, as the train was not in motion, I could catch bits of their conversation when others were not talking.

They talked first of the prices of goods and the condition of business; they referred to a person whom they both knew; then they plunged into the fair at Nijni Novgorod. The clerk boasted of knowing people who were leading a gay life there, but the old man did not allow him to continue, and, interrupting him, began to describe the festivities of the previous year at Kounavino, in which he had taken part. He was evidently proud of these recollections, and, probably thinking that this would detract nothing from the gravity which his face and manners expressed, he related with pride how, when drunk, he had fired, at Kounavino, such a broadside that he could describe it only in the other's ear.

The clerk began to laugh noisily. The old man laughed too, showing two long yellow teeth. Their conversation not interesting me, I left the car to stretch my legs. At the door I met the lawyer and his lady.

"You have no more time," the lawyer said to me. "The second bell is about to ring."

Indeed I had scarcely reached the rear of the train when the bell sounded. As I entered the car again, the lawyer was talking with his companion in an animated fashion. The merchant, sitting opposite them, was taciturn.

"And then she squarely declared to her husband," said the lawyer with a smile, as I passed by them, "that she neither could nor would live with him, because..."

And he continued, but I did not hear the rest of the sentence, my attention being distracted by the passing of the conductor and a new traveller. When silence was restored, I again heard the lawyer's voice. The conversation had passed from a special case to general considerations.

"And afterward comes discord, financial difficulties, disputes between the two parties, and the couple separate. In the good old days that seldom happened. Is it not so?" asked the lawyer of the two merchants, evidently trying to drag them into the conversation.

Just then the train started, and the old man, without answering, took off his cap, and crossed himself three times while muttering a prayer. When he had finished, he clapped his cap far down on his head, and said:

"Yes, sir, that happened in former times also, but not as often. In the present day it is bound to happen more frequently. People have become too learned."

The lawyer made some reply to the old man, but the train, ever increasing its speed, made such a clatter upon the rails that I could no longer hear distinctly. As I was interested in what the old man was saying, I drew nearer. My neighbor, the nervous gentleman, was evidently interested also, and, without changing his seat, he lent an ear.

"But what harm is there in education?" asked the lady, with a smile that was scarcely perceptible. "Would it be better to marry as in the old days, when the bride and bridegroom did not even see each other before marriage?" she continued, answering, as is the habit of our ladies, not the words that her interlocutor had spoken, but the words she believed he was going to speak. "Women did not know whether they would love or would be loved, and they were married to the first comer, and suffered all their lives. Then you think it was better so?" she continued, evidently addressing the lawyer and myself, and not at all the old man.

"People have become too learned," repeated the last, looking at the lady with contempt, and leaving her question unanswered.

"I should be curious to know how you explain the correlation between education and conjugal differences," said the lawyer, with a slight smile.

The merchant wanted to make some reply, but the lady interrupted him.

"No, those days are past."

The lawyer cut short her words:–

"Let him express his thought."

"Because there is no more fear," replied the old man.

"But how will you marry people who do not love each other? Only animals can be coupled at the will of a proprietor. But people have inclinations, attachments," the lady hastened to say, casting a glance at the lawyer, at me, and even at the clerk, who, standing up and leaning his elbow on the back of a seat, was listening to the conversation with a smile.

"You are wrong to say that, madam," said the old man. "The animals are beasts, but man has received the law."

"But, nevertheless, how is one to live with a man when there is no love?" said the lady, evidently excited by the general sympathy and attention.

"Formerly no such distinctions were made," said the old man, gravely. "Only now have they become a part of our habits. As soon as the least thing happens, the wife says: 'I release you. I am going to leave your house.' Even among the moujiks this fashion has become acclimated. 'There,' she says, 'here are your shirts and drawers. I am going off with Vanka. His hair is curlier than yours.' Just go talk with them. And yet the first rule for the wife should be fear."

The clerk looked at the lawyer, the lady, and myself, evidently repressing a smile, and all ready to deride or approve the merchant's words, according to the attitude of the others.

"What fear?" said the lady.

"This fear, – the wife must fear her husband; that is what fear."

"Oh, that, my little father, that is ended."

"No, madam, that cannot end. As she, Eve, the woman, was taken from man's ribs, so she will remain unto the end of the world," said the old man, shaking his head so triumphantly and so severely that the clerk, deciding that the victory was on his side, burst into a loud laugh.

"Yes, you men think so," replied the lady, without surrendering, and turning toward us. "You have given yourself liberty. As for woman, you wish to keep her in the seraglio. To you, everything is permissible. Is it not so?"

"Oh, man, – that's another affair."

"Then, according to you, to man everything is permissible?"

"No one gives him this permission; only, if the man behaves badly outside, the family is not increased thereby; but the woman, the wife, is a fragile vessel," continued the merchant, severely.

His tone of authority evidently subjugated his hearers. Even the lady felt crushed, but she did not surrender.

"Yes, but you will admit, I think, that woman is a human being, and has feelings like her husband. What should she do if she does not love her husband?"

"If she does not love him!" repeated the old man, stormily, and knitting his brows; "why, she will be made to love him."

This unexpected argument pleased the clerk, and he uttered a murmur of approbation.

"Oh, no, she will not be forced," said the lady. "Where there is no love, one cannot be obliged to love in spite of herself."

"And if the wife deceives her husband, what is to be done?" said the lawyer.

"That should not happen," said the old man. "He must have his eyes about him."

"And if it does happen, all the same? You will admit that it does happen?"

"It happens among the upper classes, not among us," answered the old man. "And if any husband is found who is such a fool as not to rule his wife, he will not have robbed her. But no scandal, nevertheless. Love or not, but do not disturb the household. Every husband can govern his wife. He has the necessary power. It is only the imbecile who does not succeed in doing so."

Everybody was silent. The clerk moved, advanced, and, not wishing to lag behind the others in the conversation, began with his eternal smile:

"Yes, in the house of our employer, a scandal has arisen, and it is very difficult to view the matter clearly. The wife loved to amuse herself, and began to go astray. He is a capable and serious man. First, it was with the book-keeper. The husband tried to bring her back to reason through kindness. She did not change her conduct. She plunged into all sorts of beastliness. She began to steal his money. He beat her, but she grew worse and worse. To an unbaptized, to a pagan, to a Jew (saving your permission), she went in succession for her caresses. What could the employer do? He has dropped her entirely, and now he lives as a bachelor. As for her, she is dragging in the depths."

"He is an imbecile," said the old man. "If from the first he had not allowed her to go in her own fashion, and had kept a firm hand upon her, she would be living honestly, no danger. Liberty must be taken away from the beginning. Do not trust yourself to your horse upon the highway. Do not trust yourself to your wife at home."

At that moment the conductor passed, asking for the tickets for the next station. The old man gave up his.

"Yes, the feminine sex must be dominated in season, else all will perish."

"And you yourselves, at Kounavino, did you not lead a gay life with the pretty girls?" asked the lawyer with a smile.

"Oh, that's another matter," said the merchant, severely. "Good-by," he added, rising. He wrapped himself in his cloak, lifted his cap, and, taking his bag, left the car.

# CHAPTER II

Scarcely had the old man gone when a general conversation began.

"There's a little Old Testament father for you," said the clerk.

"He is a Domostroy,"[1] said the lady. "What savage ideas about a woman and marriage!"

"Yes, gentlemen," said the lawyer, "we are still a long way from the European ideas upon marriage. First, the rights of woman, then free marriage, then divorce, as a question not yet solved..."

"The main thing, and the thing which such people as he do not understand," rejoined the lady, "is that only love consecrates marriage, and that the real marriage is that which is consecrated by love."

---

1  The Domostroy is a matrimonial code of the days of Ivan the Terrible.

The clerk listened and smiled, with the air of one accustomed to store in his memory all intelligent conversation that he hears, in order to make use of it afterwards.

"But what is this love that consecrates marriage?" said, suddenly, the voice of the nervous and taciturn gentleman, who, unnoticed by us, had approached.

He was standing with his hand on the seat, and evidently agitated. His face was red, a vein in his forehead was swollen, and the muscles of his cheeks quivered.

"What is this love that consecrates marriage?" he repeated.

"What love?" said the lady. "The ordinary love of husband and wife."

"And how, then, can ordinary love consecrate marriage?" continued the nervous gentleman, still excited, and with a displeased air. He seemed to wish to say something disagreeable to the lady. She felt it, and began to grow agitated.

"How? Why, very simply," said she.

The nervous gentleman seized the word as it left her lips.

"No, not simply."

"Madam says," interceded the lawyer indicating his companion, "that marriage should be first the result of an attachment, of a love, if you will, and that, when love exists, and in that case only, marriage represents something sacred. But every marriage which is not based on a natural attachment, on love, has in it nothing that is morally obligatory. Is not that the idea that you intended to convey?" he asked the lady.

The lady, with a nod of her head, expressed her approval of this translation of her thoughts.

"Then," resumed the lawyer, continuing his remarks.

But the nervous gentleman, evidently scarcely able to contain himself, without allowing the lawyer to finish, asked:

"Yes, sir. But what are we to understand by this love that alone consecrates marriage?"

"Everybody knows what love is," said the lady.

"But I don't know, and I should like to know how you define it."

"How? It is very simple," said the lady.

And she seemed thoughtful, and then said:

"Love . . . love . . . is a preference for one man or one woman to the exclusion of all others..."

"A preference for how long? . . . For a month, two days, or half an hour?" said the nervous gentleman, with special irritation.

"No, permit me, you evidently are not talking of the same thing."

"Yes, I am talking absolutely of the same thing. Of the preference for one man or one woman to the exclusion of all others. But I ask: a preference for how long?"

"For how long? For a long time, for a life-time sometimes."

"But that happens only in novels. In life, never. In life this preference for one to the exclusion of all others lasts in rare cases several years, oftener several months, or even weeks, days, hours..."

"Oh, sir. Oh, no, no, permit me," said all three of us at the same time.

The clerk himself uttered a monosyllable of disapproval.

"Yes, I know," he said, shouting louder than all of us; "you are talking of what is believed to exist, and I am talking of what is. Every man feels what you call love toward each pretty woman he sees, and very little toward his wife. That is the origin of the proverb, – and it is a true one, – 'Another's wife is a white swan, and ours is bitter wormwood.'"

"Ah, but what you say is terrible! There certainly exists among human beings this feeling which is called love, and which lasts, not for months and years, but for life."

"No, that does not exist. Even if it should be admitted that Menelaus had preferred Helen all his life, Helen would have preferred Paris; and so it has been, is, and will be eternally. And it cannot be otherwise, just as it cannot happen that, in a load of chick-peas, two peas marked with a special sign should fall side by side. Further, this is not only an improbability, but it is certain that a feeling of satiety will come to Helen or to Menelaus. The whole difference is that to one it comes sooner, to the other later. It is only in stupid novels that it is written that 'they loved each other all their lives.' And none but children can believe it. To talk of loving a man or woman for life is like saying that a candle can burn forever."

"But you are talking of physical love. Do you not admit a love based upon a conformity of ideals, on a spiritual affinity?"

"Why not? But in that case it is not necessary to procreate together (excuse my brutality). The point is that this conformity of ideals is not met among old people, but among young and pretty persons," said he, and he began to laugh disagreeably.

"Yes, I affirm that love, real love, does not consecrate marriage, as we are in the habit of believing, but that, on the contrary, it ruins it."

"Permit me," said the lawyer. "The facts contradict your words. We see that marriage exists, that all humanity – at least the larger portion – lives conjugally, and that many husbands and wives honestly end a long life together."

The nervous gentleman smiled ill-naturedly.

"And what then? You say that marriage is based upon love, and when I give voice to a doubt as to the existence of any other love than sensual love, you prove to me the existence of love by marriage. But in our day marriage is only a violence and falsehood."

"No, pardon me," said the lawyer. "I say only that marriages have existed and do exist."

"But how and why do they exist? They have existed, and they do exist, for people who have seen, and do see, in marriage something sacramental, a sacrament that is binding before God. For such people marriages exist, but to us they are only hypocrisy and violence. We feel it, and, to clear ourselves, we preach free love; but, really, to preach free love is only a call backward to the promiscuity of the sexes (excuse me, he said to the lady), the haphazard sin of certain raskolniks. The old foundation is shattered; we must build a new one, but we must not preach debauchery."

He grew so warm that all became silent, looking at him in astonishment.

"And yet the transition state is terrible. People feel that haphazard sin is inadmissible. It is necessary in some way or other to regulate the sexual relations; but there exists no other foundation than the old one, in which nobody longer believes? People marry in the old fashion, without believing in what they do, and the result is falsehood, violence. When it is falsehood alone, it is easily endured. The husband and wife simply deceive the world by professing to live monogamically. If they really are polygamous and polyandrous, it is bad, but acceptable. But when, as often happens, the husband and the wife have taken upon themselves the obligation to live together all their lives (they themselves do not know why), and from the second month have already a desire to separate, but continue to live together just the same, then comes that infernal existence in which they resort to drink, in which they fire revolvers, in which they assassinate each other, in which they poison each other."

All were silent, but we felt ill at ease.

"Yes, these critical episodes happen in marital life. For instance, there is the Posdnicheff affair," said the lawyer, wishing to stop the conversation on this embarrassing and too exciting ground. "Have you read how he killed his wife through jealousy?"

The lady said that she had not read it. The nervous gentleman said nothing, and changed color.

"I see that you have divined who I am," said he, suddenly, after a pause.

"No, I have not had that pleasure."

"It is no great pleasure. I am Posdnicheff."

New silence. He blushed, then turned pale again.

"What matters it, however?" said he. "Excuse me, I do not wish to embarrass you."

And he resumed his old seat.

# CHAPTER III

I resumed mine, also. The lawyer and the lady whispered together. I was sitting beside Posdnicheff, and I maintained silence. I desired to talk to him, but I did not know how to begin, and thus an hour passed until we reached the next station.

There the lawyer and the lady went out, as well as the clerk. We were left alone, Posdnicheff and I.

"They say it, and they lie, or they do not understand," said Posdnicheff.

"Of what are you talking?"

"Why, still the same thing."

He leaned his elbows upon his knees, and pressed his hands against his temples.

"Love, marriage, family, – all lies, lies, lies."

He rose, lowered the lamp-shade, lay down with his elbows on the cushion, and closed his eyes. He remained thus for a minute.

"Is it disagreeable to you to remain with me, now that you know who I am?"

"Oh, no."

"You have no desire to sleep?"

"Not at all."

"Then do you want me to tell you the story of my life?"

Just then the conductor passed. He followed him with an ill-natured look, and did not begin until he had gone again. Then during all the rest of the story he did not stop once. Even the new travellers as they entered did not stop him.

His face, while he was talking, changed several times so completely that it bore positively no resemblance to itself as it had appeared just before. His eyes, his mouth, his moustache, and even his beard, all were new. Each time it was a beautiful and touching physiognomy, and these transformations were produced suddenly in the penumbra; and for five minutes it was the same face, that could not be compared to that of five minutes before. And then, I know not how, it changed again, and became unrecognizable.

# CHAPTER IV

"Well, I am going then to tell you my life, and my whole frightful history, – yes, frightful. And the story itself is more frightful than the outcome."

He became silent for a moment, passed his hands over his eyes, and began:–

To be understood clearly, the whole must be told from the beginning. It must be told how and why I married, and what I was before my marriage. First, I will tell you who I am. The son of a rich gentleman of the steppes, an old marshal of the nobility, I was a University pupil, a graduate of the law school. I married in my thirtieth year. But before talking to you of my marriage, I must tell you how I lived formerly, and what ideas I had of conjugal life. I led the life of so many other so-called respectable people, – that is, in debauchery. And like the majority, while leading the life of a debauche, I was convinced that I was a man of irreproachable morality.

The idea that I had of my morality arose from the fact that in my family there was no knowledge of those special debaucheries, so common in the surroundings of land-owners, and also from the fact that my father and my mother did not deceive each other. In consequence of this, I had built from childhood a dream of high and poetical conjugal life. My wife was to be perfection itself, our mutual love was to be incomparable, the purity of our conjugal life stainless. I thought thus, and all the time I marvelled at the nobility of my projects.

At the same time, I passed ten years of my adult life without hurrying toward marriage, and I led what I called the well-regulated and reasonable life of a bachelor. I was proud of it before my friends, and before all men of my age who abandoned themselves to all sorts of special refinements. I was not a seducer, I had no unnatural tastes, I did not make debauchery the principal object of my life; but I found pleasure within the limits of society's rules, and innocently believed myself a profoundly moral being. The women with whom I had relations did not belong to me alone, and I asked of them nothing but the pleasure of the moment.

In all this I saw nothing abnormal. On the contrary, from the fact that I did not engage my heart, but paid in cash, I supposed that I was honest. I avoided those women who, by attaching them-selves to me, or presenting me with a child, could bind my future. Moreover, perhaps there may have been children or attachments; but I so arranged matters that I could not become aware of them.

"And living thus, I considered myself a perfectly honest man. I did not understand that debauchery does not consist simply in physical acts, that no matter what physical ignominy does not yet constitute debauchery, and that real debauchery consists in freedom from the moral bonds toward a woman with whom one enters into carnal relations, and I regarded THIS FREEDOM as a merit. I remember that I once tortured myself exceedingly for having forgotten to pay a woman who probably had given herself to me through love. I only became tranquil again when, having sent her the money, I had thus shown her that I did not consider myself as in any way bound to her. Oh, do not shake your head as if you were in agreement with me (he cried suddenly with vehemence). I know these tricks. All of you, and you especially, if you are not a rare exception, have the same ideas that I had then. If you are in agreement with me, it is now only. Formerly you did not think so. No more did I; and, if I had been told what I have just told you, that which has happened would not have happened. However, it is all the same. Excuse me (he continued): the truth is that it is frightful, frightful, frightful, this abyss of errors and debaucheries in which we live face to face with the real question of the rights of woman...."

"What do you mean by the 'real' question of the rights of woman?"

"The question of the nature of this special being, organized otherwise than man, and how this being and man ought to view the wife...."

# CHAPTER V

Yes: for ten years I lived the most revolting existence, while dreaming of the noblest love, and even in the name of that love. Yes, I want to tell you how I killed my wife, and for that I must tell you how I debauched myself. I killed her before I knew her.

I killed THE wife when I first tasted sensual joys without love, and then it was that I killed MY wife. Yes, sir: it is only after having suffered, after having tortured myself, that I have come to understand the root of things, that I have come to understand my crimes. Thus you will see where and how began the drama that has led me to misfortune.

It is necessary to go back to my sixteenth year, when I was still at school, and my elder brother a first-year student. I had not yet known women but, like all the unfortunate children of our society, I was already no longer innocent. I was tortured, as you were, I am sure, and as are tortured ninety-nine one-hundredths of our boys. I lived in a frightful dread, I prayed to God, and I prostrated myself.

I was already perverted in imagination, but the last steps remained to be taken. I could still escape, when a friend of my brother, a very gay student, one of those who are called good fellows, – that is, the greatest of scamps, – and who had taught us to drink and play cards, took advantage of a night of intoxication to drag us THERE. We started. My brother, as innocent as I, fell that night, and I, a mere lad of sixteen, polluted myself and helped to pollute a sister-woman, without understanding what I did. Never had I heard from my elders that what I thus did was bad. It is true that there are the ten commandments of the Bible; but the commandments are made only to be recited before the priests at examinations, and even then are not as exacting as the commandments in regard to the use of ut in conditional propositions.

"Thus, from my elders, whose opinion I esteemed, I had never heard that this was reprehensible. On the contrary, I had heard people whom I respected say that it was good. I had heard that my struggles and my sufferings would be appeased after this act. I had heard it and read it. I had heard from my elders that it was excellent for the health, and my friends have always seemed to believe that it contained I know not what merit and valor. So nothing is seen in it but what is praiseworthy. As for the danger of disease, it is a foreseen danger. Does not the government guard against it? And even science corrupts us."

"How so, science?" I asked.

"Why, the doctors, the pontiffs of science. Who pervert young people by laying down such rules of hygiene? Who pervert women by devising and teaching them ways by which not to have children?

Yes: if only a hundredth of the efforts spent in curing diseases were spent in curing debauchery, disease would long ago have ceased to exist, whereas now all efforts are employed, not in extirpating debauchery, but in favoring it, by assuring the harmlessness of the consequences. Besides, it is not a question of that. It is a question of this frightful thing that has happened to me, as it happens to nine-tenths, if not more, not only of the men of our society, but of all societies, even peasants, – this frightful thing that I had fallen, and not because I was subjected to the natural seduction of a certain woman. No, no woman seduced me. I fell because the surroundings in which I found myself saw in this degrading thing only a legitimate function, useful to the health; because others saw in it simply a natural amusement, not only excusable, but even innocent in a young man. I did not understand that it was a fall, and I began to give myself to those pleasures (partly from desire and partly from necessity) which I was led to believe were characteristic of my age, just as I had begun to drink and smoke.

And yet there was in this first fall something peculiar and touching. I remember that straightway I was filled with such a profound sadness that I had a desire to weep, to weep over the loss forever of my relations with woman. Yes, my relations with woman were lost forever. Pure relations with women, from that time forward, I could no longer have. I had become what is called a voluptuary; and to be a voluptuary is a physical condition like the condition of a victim of the morphine habit, of a drunkard, and of a smoker.

"Just as the victim of the morphine habit, the drunkard, the smoker, is no longer a normal man, so the man who has known several women for his pleasure is no longer normal? He is abnormal forever. He is a voluptuary. Just as the drunkard and the victim of the morphine habit may be recognized by their face and manner, so we may recognize a voluptuary. He may repress himself and struggle, but nevermore will he enjoy simple, pure, and fraternal relations toward woman. By his way of glancing at a young woman one may at once recognize a voluptuary; and I became a voluptuary, and I have remained one."

# CHAPTER VI

Yes, so it is; and that went farther and farther with all sorts of variations. My God! when I remember all my cowardly acts and bad deeds, I am frightened. And I remember that 'me' who, during that period, was still the butt of his comrades' ridicule on account of his innocence.

And when I hear people talk of the gilded youth, of the officers, of the Parisians, and all these gentlemen, and myself, living wild lives at the age of thirty, and who have on our consciences hundreds of crimes toward women, terrible and varied, when we enter a parlor or a ball-room, washed, shaven, and perfumed, with very white linen, in dress coats or in uniform, as emblems of purity, oh, the disgust! There will surely come a time, an epoch, when all these lives and all this cowardice will be unveiled!

So, nevertheless, I lived, until the age of thirty, without abandoning for a minute my intention of marrying, and building an elevated conjugal life; and with this in view I watched all young girls who might suit me. I was buried in rottenness, and at the same time I looked for virgins, whose purity was worthy of me! Many of them were rejected: they did not seem to me pure enough!

Finally I found one that I considered on a level with myself. She was one of two daughters of a landed proprietor of Penza, formerly very rich and since ruined. To tell the truth, without false modesty, they pursued me and finally captured me. The mother (the father was away) laid all sorts of traps, and one of these, a trip in a boat, decided my future.

I made up my mind at the end of the aforesaid trip one night, by moonlight, on our way home, while I was sitting beside her. I admired her slender body, whose charming shape was moulded by a jersey, and her curling hair, and I suddenly concluded that THIS WAS SHE. It seemed to me on that beautiful evening that she understood all that I thought and felt, and I thought and felt the most elevating things.

Really, it was only the jersey that was so becoming to her, and her curly hair, and also the fact that I had spent the day beside her, and that I desired a more intimate relation.

I returned home enthusiastic, and I persuaded myself that she realized the highest perfection, and that for that reason she was worthy to be my wife, and the next day I made to her a proposal of marriage.

No, say what you will, we live in such an abyss of falsehood, that, unless some event strikes us a blow on the head, as in my case, we cannot awaken. What confusion! Out of the thousands of men who marry, not only among us, but also among the people, scarcely will you find a single one who has not previously married at least ten times. (It is true that there now exist, at least so I have heard, pure young people who feel and know that this is not a joke, but a serious matter. May God come to their aid! But in my time there was not to be found one such in a thousand.)

And all know it, and pretend not to know it. In all the novels are described down to the smallest details the feelings of the characters, the lakes and brambles around which they walk; but, when it comes to describing their GREAT love, not a word is breathed of what HE, the interesting character, has previously done, not a word about his frequenting of disreputable houses, or his association with nursery-maids, cooks, and the wives of others.

"And if anything is said of these things, such IMPROPER novels are not allowed in the hands of young girls. All men have the air of believing, in presence of maidens, that these corrupt pleasures, in which EVERYBODY takes part, do not exist, or exist only to a very small extent. They pretend it so carefully that they succeed in convincing themselves of it. As for the poor young girls, they believe it quite seriously, just as my poor wife believed it.

"I remember that, being already engaged, I showed her my 'memoirs,' from which she could learn more or less of my past, and especially my last liaison which she might perhaps have discovered through the gossip of some third party. It was for this last reason, for that matter, that I felt the necessity of communicating these memoirs to her. I can still see her fright, her despair, her bewilderment, when she had learned and understood it. She was on the point of breaking the engagement. What a lucky thing it would have been for both of us!"

Posdnicheff was silent for a moment, and then resumed:–

"After all, no! It is better that things happened as they did, better!" he cried. "It was a good thing for me. Besides, it makes no difference. I was saying that in these cases it is the poor young girls who are deceived. As for the mothers, the mothers especially, informed by their husbands, they know  all, and, while pretending to believe in the purity of the young man, they act as if they did not believe in it.

They know what bait must be held out to people for themselves and their daughters. We men sin through ignorance, and a determination not to learn.  As for the women, they know very well  that the noblest and most poetic love,  as we call it, depends, not on moral qualities, but on the physical intimacy,  and also on the manner of doing the hair, and the color and shape.

Ask an experienced coquette, who has undertaken to seduce a man, which she would prefer, – to be convicted, in presence of the man whom she is engaged in conquering, of falsehood, perversity, cruelty, or to appear before  him in an ill-fitting dress, or a dress of an unbecoming color. She will prefer the first alternative. She knows very  well that we simply lie when we talk of our elevated sentiments, that we seek only the possession of her body, and that because of that we will forgive her every sort of baseness, but will not forgive her a costume of an ugly shade, without taste or fit.

And these things she knows by reason, where as the maiden knows them only by instinct, like the animal. Hence these abominable jerseys, these artificial humps on the back, these bare shoulders, arms, and throats.

Women, especially those who have passed through the school of marriage, know very well that conversations upon elevated subjects are only conversations, and that man seeks and desires the body and all that ornaments the body. Consequently, they act accordingly? If we reject conventional explanations, and view the life of our upper and lower classes as it is, with all its shamelessness, it is only a vast perversity. You do not share this opinion? Permit me, I am going to prove it to you (said he, interrupting me).

You say that the women of our society live for a different interest from that which actuates fallen women. And I say no, and I am going to prove it to you. If beings differ from one another according to the purpose of their life, according to their INNER LIFE, this will necessarily be reflected also in their OUTER LIFE, and their exterior will be very different. Well, then, compare the wretched, the despised, with the women of the highest society: the same dresses, the same fashions, the same perfumeries, the same passion for jewelry, for brilliant and very expensive articles, the same amusements, dances, music, and songs. The former attract by all possible means; so do the latter. No difference, none whatever!

"Yes, and I, too, was captivated by jerseys, bustles, and curly hair."

# CHAPTER VII

And it was very easy to capture me, since I was brought up under artificial conditions, like cucumbers in a hothouse. Our too abundant nourishment, together with complete physical idleness, is nothing but systematic excitement of the imagination. The men of our society are fed and kept like reproductive stallions. It is sufficient to close the valve, – that is, for a young man to live a quiet life for some time, – to produce as an immediate result a restlessness, which, becoming exaggerated by reflection through the prism of our unnatural life, provokes the illusion of love.

All our idyls and marriage, all, are the result for the most part of our eating. Does that astonish you? For my part, I am astonished that we do not see it. Not far from my estate this spring some moujiks were working on a railway embankment. You know what a peasant's food is, –

bread, kvass,[2] onions. With this frugal nourishment he lives, he is alert, he makes light work in the fields. But on the railway this bill of fare becomes cacha and a pound of meat. Only he restores this meat by sixteen hours of labor pushing loads weighing twelve hundred pounds.

"And we, who eat two pounds of meat and game, we who absorb all sorts of heating drinks and food, how do we expend it? In sensual excesses. If the valve is open, all goes well; but close it, as I had closed it temporarily before my marriage, and immediately there will result an excitement which, deformed by novels, verses, music, by our idle and luxurious life, will give a love of the finest water. I, too, fell in love, as everybody does, and there were transports, emotions, poesy; but really all this passion was prepared by mamma and the dressmakers. If there had been no trips in boats, no well-fitted garments, etc., if my wife had worn some shapeless blouse, and I had seen her thus

---

2   Kvass, a sort of cider.

at her home, I should not have been seduced."

# CHAPTER VIII

And note, also, this falsehood, of which all are guilty; the way in which marriages are made. What could there be more natural? The young girl is marriageable, she should marry. What simpler, provided the young person is not a monster, and men can be found with a desire to marry? Well, no, here begins a new hypocrisy.

Formerly, when the maiden arrived at a favorable age, her marriage was arranged by her parents. That was done, that is done still, throughout humanity, among the Chinese, the Hindoos, the Mussulmans, and among our common people also. Things are so managed in at least ninety-nine per cent. of the families of the entire human race.

"Only we riotous livers have imagined that this way was bad, and have invented another. And this other, – what is it? It is this. The young girls are seated, and the gentlemen walk up and down before them, as in a bazaar, and make their choice. The maidens wait and think, but do not dare to say: 'Take me, young man, me and not her. Look at these shoulders and the rest.' We males walk up and down, and estimate the merchandise, and then we discourse upon the rights of woman, upon the liberty that she acquires, I know not how, in the theatrical halls."

"But what is to be done?" said I to him. "Shall the woman make the advances?"

I do not know. But, if it is a question of equality, let the equality be complete. Though it has been found that to contract marriages through the agency of match-makers is humiliating, it is nevertheless a thousand times preferable to our system. There the rights and the chances are equal; here the woman is a slave, exhibited in the market. But as she cannot bend to her condition, or make advances herself, there begins that other and more abominable lie which is sometimes called GOING INTO SOCIETY, sometimes AMUSING ONE'S SELF, and which is really nothing but the hunt for a husband.

But say to a mother or to her daughter that they are engaged only in a hunt for a husband. God! What an offence! Yet they can do nothing else, and have nothing else to do; and the terrible feature of it all is to see sometimes very young, poor, and innocent maidens haunted solely by such ideas. If only, I repeat, it were done frankly; but it is always accompanied with lies and babble of this sort:–

'Ah, the descent of species! How interesting it is!'

'Oh, Lily is much interested in painting.'

'Shall you go to the Exposition? How charming it is!'

'And the troika, and the plays, and the symphony. Ah, how adorable!'

'My Lise is passionately fond of music.'

'And you, why do you not share these convictions?'

"And through all this verbiage, all have but one single idea: 'Take me, take my Lise. No, me! Only try!"'

# CHAPTER IX

"Do you know," suddenly continued Posdnicheff, "that this power of women from which the world suffers arises solely from what I have just spoken of?"

"What do you mean by the power of women?" I said. "Everybody, on the contrary, complains that women have not sufficient rights, that they are in subjection."

"That's it; that's it exactly," said he, vivaciously. "That is just what I mean, and that is the explanation of this extraordinary phenomenon, that on the one hand woman is reduced to the lowest degree of humiliation and on the other hand she reigns over everything. See the Jews: with their power of money, they avenge their subjection, just as the women do. 'Ah! you wish us to be only merchants? All right; remaining merchants, we will get possession of you,' say the Jews. 'Ah! you wish us to be only objects of sensuality? All right; by the aid of sensuality we will bend you beneath our yoke,' say the women."

"The absence of the rights of woman does not consist in the fact that she has not the right to vote, or the right to sit on the bench, but in the fact that in her affectional relations she is not the equal of man, she has not the right to abstain, to choose instead of being chosen. You say that that would be abnormal. Very well! But then do not let man enjoy these rights, while his companion is deprived of them, and finds herself obliged to make use of the coquetry by which she governs, so that the result is that man chooses 'formally,' whereas really it is woman who chooses. As soon as she is in possession of her means, she abuses them, and acquires a terrible supremacy."

"But where do you see this exceptional power?"

Where? Why, everywhere, in everything. Go see the stores in the large cities. There are millions there, millions. It is impossible to estimate the enormous quantity of labor that is expended there. In nine-tenths of these stores is there anything whatever for the use of men? All the luxury of life is demanded and sustained by woman. Count the factories; the greater part of them are engaged in making feminine ornaments. Millions of men, generations of slaves, die toiling like convicts simply to satisfy the whims of our companions.

Women, like queens, keep nine-tenths of the human race as prisoners of war, or as prisoners at hard labor. And all this because they have been humiliated, because they have been deprived of rights equal to those which men enjoy. They take revenge for our sensuality; they catch us in their nets.

Yes, the whole thing is there. Women have made of themselves such a weapon to act upon the senses that a young man, and even an old man, cannot remain tranquil in their presence. Watch a popular festival, or our receptions or ball-rooms. Woman well knows her influence there. You will see it in her triumphant smiles.

As soon as a young man advances toward a woman, directly he falls under the influence of this opium, and loses his head. Long ago I felt ill at ease when I saw a woman too well adorned, – whether a woman of the people with her red neckerchief and her looped skirt, or a woman of our own society in her ball-room dress. But now it simply terrifies me. I see in it a danger to men, something contrary to the laws; and I feel a desire to call a policeman, to appeal for defence from some quarter, to demand that this dangerous object be removed.

"And this is not a joke, by any means. I am convinced, I am sure, that the time will come – and perhaps it is not far distant – when the world will understand this, and will be astonished that a society could exist in which actions as harmful as those which appeal to sensuality by adorning the body as our companions do were allowed. As well set traps along our public streets, or worse than that."

# CHAPTER X

That, then, was the way in which I was captured. I was in love, as it is called; not only did she appear to me a perfect being, but I considered myself a white blackbird. It is a commonplace fact that there is no one so low in the world that he cannot find some one viler than himself, and consequently puff with pride and self-contentment. I was in that situation. I did not marry for money. Interest was foreign to the affair, unlike the marriages of most of my acquaintances, who married either for money or for relations. First, I was rich, she was poor. Second, I was especially proud of the fact that, while others married with an intention of continuing their polygamic life as bachelors, it was my firm intention to live monogamically after my engagement and the wedding, and my pride swelled immeasurably.

Yes, I was a wretch, convinced that I was an angel. The period of my engagement did not last long. I cannot remember those days without shame. What an abomination!

It is generally agreed that love is a moral sentiment, a community of thought rather than of sense. If that is the case, this community of thought ought to find expression in words and conversation. Nothing of the sort. It was extremely difficult for us to talk with each other. What a toil of Sisyphus was our conversation! Scarcely had we thought of something to say, and said it, when we had to resume our silence and try to discover new subjects. Literally, we did not know what to say to each other. All that we could think of concerning the life that was before us and our home was said.

And then what? If we had been animals, we should have known that we had not to talk. But here, on the contrary, it was necessary to talk, and there were no resources! For that which occupied our minds was not a thing to be expressed in words.

And then that silly custom of eating bon-bons, that brutal gluttony for sweetmeats, those abominable preparations for the wedding, those discussions with mamma upon the apartments, upon the sleeping-rooms, upon the bedding, upon the morning-gowns, upon the wrappers, the linen, the costumes! Understand that if people married according to the old fashion, as this old man said just now, then these eiderdown coverlets and this bedding would all be sacred details; but with us, out of ten married people there is scarcely to be found one who, I do not say believes in sacraments (whether he believes or not is a matter of indifference to us), but believes in what he promises. Out of a hundred men, there is scarcely one who has not married before, and out of fifty scarcely one who has not made up his mind to deceive his wife.

"The great majority look upon this journey to the church as a condition necessary to the possession of a certain woman. Think then of the supreme significance which material details must take on. Is it not a sort of sale, in which a maiden is given over to a debauche, the sale being surrounded with the most agreeable details?"

# CHAPTER XI

All marry in this way. And I did like the rest. If the young people who dream of the honeymoon only knew what a disillusion it is, and always a disillusion! I really do not know why all think it necessary to conceal it.

One day I was walking among the shows in Paris, when, attracted by a sign, I entered an establishment to see a bearded woman and a water-dog. The woman was a man in disguise, and the dog was an ordinary dog, covered with a sealskin, and swimming in a bath. It was not in the least interesting, but the Barnum accompanied me to the exit very courteously, and, in addressing the people who were coming in, made an appeal to my testimony. 'Ask the gentleman if it is not worth seeing! Come in, come in! It only costs a franc!' And in my confusion I did not dare to answer that there was nothing curious to be seen, and it was upon my false shame that the Barnum must have counted.

It must be the same with the persons who have passed through the abominations of the honeymoon. They do not dare to undeceive their neighbor. And I did the same.

"The felicities of the honeymoon do not exist. On the contrary, it is a period of uneasiness, of shame, of pity, and, above all, of ennui, – of ferocious ennui. It is something like the feeling of a youth when he is beginning to smoke. He desires to vomit; he drivels, and swallows his drivel, pretending to enjoy this little amusement. The vice of marriage . . ."

"What! Vice?" I said. "But you are talking of one of the most natural things."

"Natural!" said he. Natural! No, I consider on the contrary that it is against nature, and it is I, a perverted man, who have reached this conviction. What would it be, then, if I had not known corruption? To a young girl, to every unperverted young girl, it is an act extremely unnatural, just as it is to children. My sister married, when very young, a man twice her own age, and who was utterly corrupt. I remember how astonished we were the night of her wedding, when, pale and covered with tears, she fled from her husband, her whole body trembling, saying that for nothing in the world would she tell what he wanted of her.

"You say natural? It is natural to eat; that is a pleasant, agreeable function, which no one is ashamed to perform from the time of his birth. No, it is not natural. A pure young girl wants one thing, — children. Children, yes, not a lover..."

"But," said I, with astonishment, "how would the human race continue?"

"But what is the use of its continuing?" he rejoined, vehemently.

"What! What is the use? But then we should not exist."

"And why is it necessary that we should exist?"

"Why, to live, to be sure."

"And why live? The Schopenhauers, the Hartmanns, and all the Buddhists, say that the greatest happiness is Nirvana, Non-Life; and they are right in this sense, – that human happiness is coincident with the annihilation of 'Self.' Only they do not express themselves well. They say that Humanity should annihilate itself to avoid its sufferings, that its object should be to destroy itself. Now the object of Humanity cannot be to avoid sufferings by annihilation, since suffering is the result of activity. The object of activity cannot consist in suppressing its consequences. The object of Man, as of Humanity, is happiness, and, to attain it, Humanity has a law which it must carry out. This law consists in the union of beings. This union is thwarted by the passions. And that is why, if the passions disappear, the union will be accomplished. Humanity then will have carried out the law, and will have no further reason to exist."

"And before Humanity carries out the law?"

"In the meantime it will have the sign of the unfulfilled law, and the existence of physical love. As long as this love shall exist, and because of it, generations will be born, one of which will finally fulfil the law. When at last the law shall be fulfilled, the Human Race will be annihilated. At least it is impossible for us to conceive of Life in the perfect union of people."

# CHAPTER XII

"Strange theory!" cried I.

Strange in what? According to all the doctrines of the Church, the world will have an end. Science teaches the same fatal conclusions. Why, then, is it strange that the same thing should result from moral Doctrine? 'Let those who can, contain,' said Christ. And I take this passage literally, as it is written. That morality may exist between people in their worldly relations, they must make complete chastity their object. In tending toward this end, man humiliates himself. When he shall reach the last degree of humiliation, we shall have moral marriage.

But if man, as in our society, tends only toward physical love, though he may clothe it with pretexts and the false forms of marriage, he will have only permissible debauchery, he will know only the same immoral life in which I fell and caused my wife to fall, a life which we call the honest life of the family. Think what a perversion of ideas must arise when the happiest situation of man, liberty, chastity, is looked upon as something wretched and ridiculous. The highest ideal, the best situation of woman, to be pure, to be a vestal, a virgin, excites fear and laughter in our society. How many, how many young girls sacrifice their purity to this Moloch of opinion by marrying rascals that they may not remain virgins, – that is, superiors! Through fear of finding themselves in that ideal state, they ruin themselves.

But I did not understand formerly, I did not understand that the words of the Gospel, that 'he who looks upon a woman to lust after her has already committed adultery,' do not apply to the wives of others, but notably and especially to our own wives. I did not understand this, and I thought that the honeymoon and all of my acts during that period were virtuous, and that to satisfy one's desires with his wife is an eminently chaste thing. Know, then, that I consider these departures, these isolations, which young married couples arrange with the permission of their parents, as nothing else than a license to engage in debauchery.

I saw, then, in this nothing bad or shameful, and, hoping for great joys, I began to live the honeymoon. And very certainly none of these joys followed. But I had faith, and was determined to have them, cost what they might. But the more I tried to secure them, the less I succeeded. All this time I felt anxious, ashamed, and weary. Soon I began to suffer. I believe that on the third or fourth day I found my wife sad and asked her the reason. I began to embrace her, which in my opinion was all that she could desire. She put me away with her hand, and began to weep.

At what? She could not tell me. She was filled with sorrow, with anguish. Probably her tortured nerves had suggested to her the truth about the baseness of our relations, but she found no words in which to say it. I began to question her; she answered that she missed her absent mother. It seemed to me that she was not telling the truth. I sought to console her by maintaining silence in regard to her parents. I did not imagine that she felt herself simply overwhelmed, and that her parents had nothing to do with her sorrow. She did not listen to me, and I accused her of caprice. I began to laugh at her gently. She dried her tears, and began to reproach me, in hard and wounding terms, for my selfishness and cruelty.

I looked at her. Her whole face expressed hatred, and hatred of me. I cannot describe to you the fright which this sight gave me. 'How? What?' thought I, 'love is the unity of souls, and here she hates me? Me? Why? But it is impossible! It is no longer she!'

I tried to calm her. I came in conflict with an immovable and cold hostility, so that, having no time to reflect, I was seized with keen irritation. We exchanged disagreeable remarks. The impression of this first quarrel was terrible. I say quarrel, but the term is inexact. It was the sudden discovery of the abyss that had been dug between us. Love was exhausted with the satisfaction of sensuality. We stood face to face in our true light, like two egoists trying to procure the greatest possible enjoyment, like two individuals trying to mutually exploit each other.

So what I called our quarrel was our actual situation as it appeared after the satisfaction of sensual desire. I did not realize that this cold hostility was our normal state, and that this first quarrel would soon be drowned under a new flood of the intensest sensuality. I thought that we had disputed with each other, and had become reconciled, and that it would not happen again. But in this same honeymoon there came a period of satiety, in which we ceased to be necessary to each other, and a new quarrel broke out.

It became evident that the first was not a matter of chance. 'It was inevitable,' I thought. This second quarrel stupefied me the more, because it was based on an extremely unjust cause. It was something like a question of money, – and never had

I haggled on that score; it was even impossible that I should do so in relation to her. I only remember that, in answer to some remark that I made, she insinuated that it was my intention to rule her by means of money, and that it was upon money that I based my sole right over her. In short, something extraordinarily stupid and base, which was neither in my character nor in hers.

I was beside myself. I accused her of indelicacy. She made the same accusation against me, and the dispute broke out. In her words, in the expression of her face, of her eyes, I noticed again the hatred that had so astonished me before. With a brother, friends, my father, I had occasionally quarrelled, but never had there been between us this fierce spite. Some time passed. Our mutual hatred was again concealed beneath an access of sensual desire, and I again consoled myself with the reflection that these scenes were reparable faults.

But when they were repeated a third and a fourth time, I understood that they were not simply faults, but a fatality that must happen again. I was no longer frightened, I was simply astonished that I should be precisely the one to live so uncomfortably with my wife, and that the same thing did not happen in other households. I did not know that in all households the same sudden changes take place, but that all, like myself, imagine that it is a misfortune exclusively reserved for themselves alone, which they carefully conceal as shameful, not only to others, but to themselves, like a bad disease.

That was what happened to me. Begun in the early days, it continued and increased with characteristics of fury that were ever more pronounced. At the bottom of my soul, from the first weeks, I felt that I was in a trap, that I had what I did not expect, and that marriage is not a joy, but a painful trial. Like everybody else, I refused to confess it (I should not have confessed it even now but for the outcome). Now I am astonished to think that I did not see my real situation. It was so easy to perceive it, in view of those quarrels, begun for reasons so trivial that afterwards one could not recall them.

Just as it often happens among gay young people that, in the absence of jokes, they laugh at their own laughter, so we found no reasons for our hatred, and we hated each other because hatred was naturally boiling up in us. More extraordinary still was the absence of causes for reconciliation.

Sometimes words, explanations, or even tears, but sometimes, I remember, after insulting words, there tacitly followed embraces and declarations. Abomination! Why is it that I did not then perceive this baseness?"

# CHAPTER XIII

All of us, men and women, are brought up in these aberrations of feeling that we call love. I from childhood had prepared myself for this thing, and I loved, and I loved during all my youth, and I was joyous in loving. It had been put into my head that it was the noblest and highest occupation in the world. But when this expected feeling came at last, and I, a man, abandoned myself to it, the lie was pierced through and through. Theoretically a lofty love is conceivable; practically it is an ignoble and degrading thing, which it is equally disgusting to talk about and to remember. It is not in vain that nature has made ceremonies, but people pretend that the ignoble and the shameful is beautiful and lofty.

I will tell you brutally and briefly what were the first signs of my love. I abandoned myself to beastly excesses, not only not ashamed of them, but proud of them, giving no thought to the intellectual life of my wife. And not only did I not think of her intellectual life, I did not even consider her physical life.

I was astonished at the origin of our hostility, and yet how clear it was! This hostility is nothing but a protest of human nature against the beast that enslaves it. It could not be otherwise. This hatred was the hatred of accomplices in a crime. Was it not a crime that, this poor woman having become pregnant in the first month, our liaison should have continued just the same?

You imagine that I am wandering from my story. Not at all. I am always giving you an account of the events that led to the murder of my wife. The imbeciles! They think that I killed my wife on the 5th of October. It was long before that that I immolated her, just as they all kill now. Understand well that in our society there is an idea shared by all that woman procures man pleasure (and vice versa, probably, but I know nothing of that, I only know my own case). Wein, Weiber und Gesang. So say the poets in their verses: Wine, women, and song!

If it were only that! Take all the poetry, the painting, the sculpture, beginning with Pouschkine's 'Little Feet,' with 'Venus and Phryne,' and you will see that woman is only a means of enjoyment. That is what she is at Trouba,[3] at Gratchevka, and in a court ball-room. And think of this diabolical trick: if she were a thing without moral value, it might be said that woman is a fine morsel; but, in the first place, these knights assure us that they adore woman (they adore her and look upon her, however, as a means of enjoyment), then all assure us that they esteem woman. Some give up their seats to her, pick up her handkerchief; others recognize in her a right to fill all offices, participate in government, etc., but, in spite of all that, the essential point remains the same. She is, she remains, an object of sensual desire, and she knows it. It is slavery, for slavery is nothing else than the utilization of the labor of some for the enjoyment of others. That slavery may not exist people must refuse to enjoy the labor of others, and

---

3  A suburb of Moscow.

look upon it as a shameful act and as a sin.

Actually, this is what happens. They abolish the external form, they suppress the formal sales of slaves, and then they imagine and assure others that slavery is abolished. They are unwilling to see that it still exists, since people, as before, like to profit by the labor of others, and think it good and just. This being given, there will always be found beings stronger or more cunning than others to profit thereby. The same thing happens in the emancipation of woman. At bottom feminine servitude consists entirely in her assimilation with a means of pleasure. They excite woman, they give her all sorts of rights equal to those of men, but they continue to look upon her as an object of sensual desire, and thus they bring her up from infancy and in public opinion.

She is always the humiliated and corrupt serf, and man remains always the debauched Master. Yes, to abolish slavery, public opinion must admit that it is shameful to exploit one's neighbor, and, to make woman free, public opinion must admit that it is shameful to consider woman as an instrument of pleasure.

"The emancipation of woman is not to be effected in the public courts or in the chamber of deputies, but in the sleeping chamber. Prostitution is to be combated, not in the houses of ill-fame, but in the family. They free woman in the public courts and in the chamber of deputies, but she remains an instrument. Teach her, as she is taught among us, to look upon herself as such, and she will always remain an inferior being. Either, with the aid of the rascally doctors, she will try to prevent conception, and descend, not to the level of an animal, but to the level of a thing; or she will be what she is in the great majority of cases, – sick, hysterical, wretched, without hope of spiritual progress..."

"But why that?" I asked.

Oh! the most astonishing thing is that no one is willing to see this thing, evident as it is, which the doctors must understand, but which they take good care not to do. Man does not wish to know the law of nature, – children. But children are born and become an embarrassment. Then man devises means of avoiding this embarrassment. We have not yet reached the low level of Europe, nor Paris, nor the 'system of two children,' nor Mahomet. We have discovered nothing, because we have given it no thought. We feel that there is something bad in the two first means; but we wish to preserve the family, and our view of woman is still worse.

With us woman must be at the same time mistress and nurse, and her strength is not sufficient. That is why we have hysteria, nervous attacks, and, among the peasants, witchcraft. Note that among the young girls of the peasantry this state of things does not exist, but only among the wives, and the wives who live with their husbands. The reason is clear, and this is the cause of the intellectual and moral decline of woman, and of her abasement.

"If they would only reflect what a grand work for the wife is the period of gestation! In her is forming the being who continues us, and this holy work is thwarted and rendered painful . . . by what? It is frightful to think of it! And after that they talk of the liberties and the rights of woman! It is like the cannibals fattening their prisoners in order to devour them, and assuring these unfortunates at the same time that their rights and their liberties are guarded!"

All this was new to me, and astonished me very much.

"But if this is so," said I, "it follows that one may love his wife only once every two years; and as man..."

And as man has need of her, you are going to say. At least, so the priests of science assure us. I would force these priests to fulfil the function of these women, who, in their opinion, are necessary to man. I wonder what song they would sing then. Assure man that he needs brandy, tobacco, opium, and he will believe those poisons necessary. It follows that God did not know how to arrange matters properly, since, without asking the opinions of the priests, he has combined things as they are. Man needs, so they have decided, to satisfy his sensual desire, and here this function is disturbed by the birth and the nursing of children.

What, then, is to be done? Why, apply to the priests; they will arrange everything, and they have really discovered a way. When, then, will these rascals with their lies be uncrowned! It is high time. We have had enough of them. People go mad, and shoot each other with revolvers, and always because of that! And how could it be otherwise?

One would say that the animals know that descent continues their race, and that they follow a certain law in regard thereto. Only man does not know this, and is unwilling to know it. He cares only to have as much sensual enjoyment as possible. The king of nature, – man! In the name of his love he kills half the human race. Of woman, who ought to be his aid in the movement of humanity toward liberty, he makes, in the name of his pleasures, not an aid, but an enemy. Who is it that everywhere puts a check upon the progressive movement of humanity? Woman. Why is it so?

"For the reason that I have given, and for that reason only."

# CHAPTER XIV

Yes, much worse than the animal is man when he does not live as a man. Thus was I. The horrible part is that I believed, inasmuch as I did not allow myself to be seduced by other women that I was leading an honest family life, that I was a very mortal being, and that if we had quarrels, the fault was in my wife, and in her character.

But it is evident that the fault was not in her. She was like everybody else, like the majority. She was brought up according to the principles exacted by the situation of our society, – that is, as all the young girls of our wealthy classes, without exception, are brought up, and as they cannot fail to be brought up. How many times we hear or read of reflections upon the abnormal condition of women, and upon what they ought to be. But these are only vain words. The education of women results from the real and not imaginary view which the world entertains of women's vocation. According to this view, the condition of women consists in procuring pleasure and it is to that end that her education is directed. From her infancy she is taught only those things that are calculated to increase her charm. Every young girl is accustomed to think only of that.

As the serfs were brought up solely to please their masters, so woman is brought up to attract men. It cannot be otherwise. But you will say, perhaps, that that applies only to young girls who are badly brought up, but that there is another education, an education that is serious, in the schools, an education in the dead languages, an education in the institutions of midwifery, an education in medical courses, and in other courses. It is false.

Every sort of feminine education has for its sole object the attraction of men.

Some attract by music or curly hair, others by science or by civic virtue. The object is the same, and cannot be otherwise (since no other object exists), – to seduce man in order to possess him.

Imagine courses of instruction for women and feminine science without men, – that is, learned women, and men not KNOWING them as learned. Oh, no! No education, no instruction can change woman as long as her highest ideal shall be marriage and not virginity, freedom from sensuality. Until that time she will remain a serf. One need only imagine, forgetting the universality of the case, the conditions in which our young girls are brought up, to avoid astonishment at the debauchery of the women of our upper classes. It is the opposite that would cause astonishment.

Follow my reasoning. From infancy garments, ornaments, cleanliness, grace, dances, music, reading of poetry, novels, singing, the theatre, the concert, for use within and without, according as women listen, or practice themselves. With that, complete physical idleness, an excessive care of the body, a vast consumption of sweetmeats; and God knows how the poor maidens suffer from their own sensuality, excited by all these things. Nine out of ten are tortured intolerably during the first period of maturity, and afterward provided they do not marry at the age of twenty. That is what we are unwilling to see, but those who have eyes see it all the same. And even the majority of these unfortunate creatures are so excited by a hidden sensuality (and it is lucky if it is hidden) that they are fit for nothing. They become animated only in the presence of men. Their whole life is spent in preparations for coquetry, or in coquetry itself. In the presence of men they become too animated; they begin to live by sensual energy. But the moment the man goes away, the life stops.

And that, not in the presence of a certain man, but in the presence of any man, provided he is not utterly hideous. You will say that this is an exception. No, it is a rule. Only in some it is made very evident, in other less so. But no one lives by her own life; they are all dependent upon man. They cannot be otherwise, since to them the attraction of the greatest number of men is the ideal of life (young girls and married women), and it is for this reason that they have no feeling stronger than that of the animal need of every female who tries to attract the largest number of males in order to increase the opportunities for choice. So it is in the life of young girls, and so it continues during marriage. In the life of young girls it is necessary in order to selection, and in marriage it is necessary in order to rule the husband. Only one thing suppresses or interrupts these tendencies for a time, – namely, children, – and then only when the woman is not a monster, – that is, when she nurses her own children. Here again the doctor interferes.

"With my wife, who desired to nurse her own children, and who did nurse six of them, it happened that the first child was sickly. The doctors, who cynically undressed her and felt of her everywhere, and whom I had to thank and pay for these acts, – these dear doctors decided that she ought not to nurse her child, and she was temporarily deprived of the only remedy for coquetry. A nurse finished the nursing of this first-born, – that is to say, we profited by the poverty and ignorance of a woman to steal her from her own little one in favor of ours, and for that purpose we dressed her in a kakoschnik trimmed with gold lace. Nevertheless, that is not the question; but there was again awakened in my wife that coquetry which had been sleeping during the nursing period. Thanks to that, she reawakened in me the torments of jealousy which I had formerly known, though in a much slighter degree."

# CHAPTER XV

Yes, jealousy, that is another of the secrets of marriage known to all and concealed by all. Besides the general cause of the mutual hatred of husbands and wives resulting from complicity in the pollution of a human being, and also from other causes, the inexhaustible source of marital wounds is jealousy. But by tacit consent it is determined to conceal them from all, and we conceal them. Knowing them, each one supposes in himself that it is an unfortunate peculiarity, and not a common destiny. So it was with me, and it had to be so. There cannot fail to be jealousy between husbands and wives who live immorally. If they cannot sacrifice their pleasures for the welfare of their child, they conclude therefrom, and truly, that they will not sacrifice their pleasures for, I will not say happiness and tranquillity (since one may sin in secret), but even for the sake of conscience. Each one knows very well that neither admits any high moral reasons for not betraying the other, since in their mutual relations they fail in the requirements of morality, and from that time distrust and watch each other.

Oh, what a frightful feeling of jealousy! I do not speak of that real jealousy which has foundations (it is tormenting, but it promises an issue), but of that unconscious jealousy which inevitably accompanies every immoral marriage, and which, having no cause, has no end. This jealousy is frightful. Frightful, that is the word.

And this is it. A young man speaks to my wife. He looks at her with a smile, and, as it seems to me, he surveys her body. How does he dare to think of her, to think of the possibility of a romance with her? And how can she, seeing this, tolerate him? Not only does she tolerate him, but she seems pleased. I even see that she puts herself to trouble on his account. And in my soul there rises such a hatred for her that each of her words, each gesture, disgusts me. She notices it, she knows not what to do, and how assume an air of indifferent animation? Ah! I suffer! That makes her gay, she is content. And my hatred increases tenfold, but I do not dare to give it free force, because at the bottom of my soul I know that there are no real reasons for it, and I remain in my seat, feigning indifference, and exaggerating my attention and courtesy to HIM.

Then I get angry with myself. I desire to leave the room, to leave them alone, and I do, in fact, go out; but scarcely am I outside when I am invaded by a fear of what is taking place within my absence. I go in again, inventing some pretext. Or sometimes I do not go in; I remain near the door, and listen. How can she humiliate herself and humiliate me by placing me in this cowardly situation of suspicion and espionage? Oh, abomination! Oh, the wicked animal! And he too, what does he think of you? But he is like all men. He is what I was before my marriage. It gives him pleasure. He even smiles when he looks at me, as much as to say: 'What have you to do with this? It is my turn now.'

This feeling is horrible. Its burn is unendurable. To entertain this feeling toward any one, to once suspect a man of lusting after my wife, was enough to spoil this man forever in my eyes, as if he had been sprinkled with vitriol. Let me once become jealous of a being, and nevermore could I re-establish with him simple human relations, and my eyes flashed when I looked at him.

As for my wife, so many times had I enveloped her with this moral vitriol, with this jealous hatred, that she was degraded thereby. In the periods of this causeless hatred I gradually uncrowned her. I covered her with shame in my imagination.

I invented impossible knaveries. I suspected, I am ashamed to say, that she, this queen of 'The Thousand and One Nights,' deceived me with my serf, under my very eyes, and laughing at me.

Thus, with each new access of jealousy (I speak always of causeless jealousy),

I entered into the furrow dug formerly by my filthy suspicions, and I continually deepened it. She did the same thing. If I have reasons to be jealous, she who knew my past had a thousand times more. And she was more ill-natured in her jealousy than I. And the sufferings that I felt from her jealousy were different, and likewise very painful.

The situation may be described thus. We are living more or less tranquilly. I am even gay and contented. Suddenly we start a conversation on some most commonplace subject, and directly she finds herself disagreeing with me upon matters concerning which we have been generally in accord. And furthermore I see that, without any necessity therefor, she is becoming irritated. I think that she has a nervous attack, or else that the subject of conversation is really disagreeable to her. We talk of something else, and that begins again. Again she torments me, and becomes irritated. I am astonished and look for a reason. Why? For what? She keeps silence, answers me with monosyllables, evidently making allusions to something. I begin to divine that the reason of all this is that I have taken a few walks in the garden with her cousin, to whom I did not give even a thought. I begin to divine, but I cannot say so. If I say so, I confirm her suspicions. I interrogate her, I question her. She does not answer, but she sees that I understand, and that confirms her suspicions.

'What is the matter with you?' I ask.

'Nothing, I am as well as usual,' she answers.

And at the same time, like a crazy woman, she gives utterance to the silliest remarks, to the most inexplicable explosions of spite.

Sometimes I am patient, but at other times I break out with anger. Then her own irritation is launched forth in a flood of insults, in charges of imaginary crimes and all carried to the highest degree by sobs, tears, and retreats through the house to the most improbable spots. I go to look for her. I am ashamed before people, before the children, but there is nothing to be done. She is in a condition where I feel that she is ready for anything. I run, and finally find her. Nights of torture follow, in which both of us, with exhausted nerves, appease each other, after the most cruel words and accusations.

"Yes, jealousy, causeless jealousy, is the condition of our debauched conjugal life. And throughout my marriage never did I cease to feel it and to suffer from it. There were two periods in which I suffered most intensely. The first time was after the birth of our first child, when the doctors had forbidden my wife to nurse it. I was particularly jealous, in the first place, because my wife felt that restlessness peculiar to animal matter when the regular course of life is interrupted without occasion. But especially was I jealous because, having seen with what facility she had thrown off her moral duties as a mother, I concluded rightly, though unconsciously, that she would throw off as easily her conjugal duties, feeling all the surer of this because she was in perfect health, as was shown by the fact that, in spite of the prohibition of the dear doctors, she nursed her following children, and even very well."

"I see that you have no love for the doctors," said I, having noticed Posdnicheff's extraordinarily spiteful expression of face and tone of voice whenever he spoke of them.

It is not a question of loving them or of not loving them. They have ruined my life, as they have ruined the lives of thousands of beings before me, and I cannot help connecting the consequence with the cause. I conceive that they desire, like the lawyers and the rest, to make money. I would willingly have given them half of my income – and any one would have done it in my place, understanding what they do – if they had consented not to meddle in my conjugal life, and to keep themselves at a distance. I have compiled no statistics, but I know scores of cases – in reality, they are innumerable – where they have killed, now a child in its mother's womb, asserting positively that the mother could not give birth to it (when the mother could give birth to it very well), now mothers, under the pretext of a so-called operation. No one has counted these murders, just as no one counted the murders of the Inquisition, because it was supposed that they were committed for the benefit of humanity. Innumerable are the crimes of the doctors! But all these crimes are nothing compared with the materialistic demoralization which they introduce into the world through women. I say nothing of the fact that, if it were to follow their advice, – thanks to the microbe which they see everywhere, – humanity, instead of tending to union, would proceed straight to complete disunion. Everybody, according to their doctrine, should isolate himself, and never remove from his mouth a syringe filled with phenic acid (moreover, they have found out now that it does no good). But I would pass over all these things. The supreme poison is the perversion of people, especially of women. One can no longer say now: 'You live badly, live better.' One can no longer say it either to himself or to others, for, if you live badly (say the doctors), the cause is in the nervous system or in something similar, and it is necessary to go to consult them, and they will prescribe for you thirty-five copecks' worth of remedies to be bought at the drug-store, and you must swallow them. Your condition grows worse? Again to the doctors, and more remedies! An excellent business!

"But to return to our subject. I was saying that my wife nursed her children well, that the nursing and the gestation of the children, and the children in general, quieted my tortures of jealousy, but that, on the other hand, they provoked torments of a different sort."

# CHAPTER XVI

The children came rapidly, one after another, and there happened what happens in our society with children and doctors. Yes, children, maternal love, it is a painful thing. Children, to a woman of our society, are not a joy, a pride, nor a fulfilment of her vocation, but a cause of fear, anxiety, and interminable suffering, torture. Women say it, they think it, and they feel it too. Children to them are really a torture, not because they do not wish to give birth to them, nurse them, and care for them (women with a strong maternal instinct – and such was my wife – are ready to do that), but because the children may fall sick and die. They do not wish to give birth to them, and then not love them; and when they love, they do not wish to feel fear for the child's health and life. That is why they do not wish to nurse them. 'If I nurse it,' they say, 'I shall become too fond of it.' One would think that they preferred india-rubber children, which could neither be sick nor die, and could always be repaired. What an entanglement in the brains of these poor women! Why such abominations to avoid pregnancy, and to avoid the love of the little ones?

Love, the most joyous condition of the soul, is represented as a danger. And why? Because, when a man does not live as a man, he is worse than a beast. A woman cannot look upon a child otherwise than as a pleasure. It is true that it is painful to give birth to it, but what little hands! . . . Oh, the little hands! Oh, the little feet! Oh, its smile! Oh, its little body! Oh, its prattle! Oh, its hiccough! In a word, it is a feeling of animal, sensual maternity. But as for any idea as to the mysterious significance of the appearance of a new human being to replace us, there is scarcely a sign of it.

Nothing of it appears in all that is said and done. No one has any faith now in a baptism of the child, and yet that was nothing but a reminder of the human significance of the newborn babe.

"They have rejected all that, but they have not replaced it, and there remain only the dresses, the laces, the little hands, the little feet, and whatever exists in the animal. But the animal has neither imagination, nor foresight, nor reason, nor a doctor.

No! not even a doctor! The chicken droops its head, overwhelmed, or the calf dies; the hen clucks and the cow lows for a time, and then these beasts continue to live, forgetting what has happened.

"With us, if the child falls sick, what is to be done, how to care for it, what doctor to call, where to go? If it dies, there will be no more little hands or little feet, and then what is the use of the sufferings endured? The cow does not ask all that, and this is why children are a source of misery. The cow has no imagination, and for that reason cannot think how it might have saved the child if it had done this or that, and its grief, founded in its physical being, lasts but a very short time. It is only a condition, and not that sorrow which becomes exaggerated to the point of despair, thanks to idleness and satiety. The cow has not that reasoning faculty which would enable it to ask the why. Why endure all these tortures? What was the use of so much love, if the little ones were to die? The cow has no logic which tells it to have no more children, and, if any come accidentally, to neither love nor nurse them, that it may not suffer. But our wives reason, and reason in this way, and that is why I said that, when a man does not live as a man, he is beneath the animal."

"But then, how is it necessary to act, in your opinion, in order to treat children humanly?" I asked.

"How? Why, love them humanly."

"Well, do not mothers love their children?"

They do not love them humanly, or very seldom do, and that is why they do not love them even as dogs. Mark this, a hen, a goose, a wolf, will always remain to woman inaccessible ideals of animal love.

It is a rare thing for a woman to throw herself, at the peril of her life, upon an elephant to snatch her child away, whereas a hen or a sparrow will not fail to fly at a dog and sacrifice itself utterly for its children. Observe this, also. Woman has the power to limit her physical love for her children, which an animal cannot do. Does that mean that, because of this, woman is inferior to the animal? No. She is superior (and even to say superior is unjust, she is not superior, she is different), but she has other duties, human duties. She can restrain herself in the matter of animal love, and transfer her love to the soul of the child. That is what woman's role should be, and that is precisely what we do not see in our society. We read of the heroic acts of mothers who sacrifice their children in the name of a superior idea, and these things seem to us like tales of the ancient world, which do not concern us. And yet I believe that, if the mother has not some ideal, in the name of which she can sacrifice the animal feeling, and if this force finds no employment, she will transfer it to chimerical attempts to physically preserve her child, aided in this task by the doctor, and she will suffer as she does suffer.

So it was with my wife. Whether there was one child or five, the feeling remained the same. In fact, it was a little better when there had been five. Life was always poisoned with fear for the children, not only from their real or imaginary diseases, but even by their simple presence. For my part, at least, throughout my conjugal life, all my interests and all my happiness depended upon the health of my children, their condition, their studies. Children, it is needless to say, are a serious consideration; but all ought to live, and in our days parents can no longer live. Regular life does not exist for them. The whole life of the family hangs by a hair. What a terrible thing it is to suddenly receive the news that little Basile is vomiting, or that Lise has a cramp in the stomach! Immediately you abandon everything, you forget everything, everything becomes nothing. The essential thing is the doctor, the enema, the temperature. You cannot begin a conversation but little Pierre comes running in with an anxious air to ask if he may eat an apple, or what jacket he shall put on, or else it is the servant who enters with a screaming baby.

Regular, steady family life does not exist. Where you live, and consequently what you do, depends upon the health of the little ones, the health of the little ones depends upon nobody, and, thanks to the doctors, who pretend to aid health, your entire life is disturbed. It is a perpetual peril. Scarcely do we believe ourselves out of it when a new danger comes: more attempts to save. Always the situation of sailors on a foundering vessel. Sometimes it seemed to me that this was done on purpose, that my wife feigned anxiety in order to conquer me, since that solved the question so simply for her benefit. It seemed to me that all that she did at those times was done for its effect upon me, but now I see that she herself, my wife, suffered and was tortured on account of the little ones, their health, and their diseases.

A torture to both of us, but to her the children were also a means of forgetting herself, like an intoxication. I often noticed, when she was very sad, that she was relieved, when a child fell sick, at being able to take refuge in this intoxication. It was involuntary intoxication, because as yet there was nothing else. On every side we heard that Mrs. So-and-so had lost children, that Dr. So-and-so had saved the child of Mrs. So-and-so, and that in a certain family all had moved from the house in which they were living, and thereby saved the little ones. And the doctors, with a serious air, confirmed this, sustaining my wife in her opinions. She was not prone to fear, but the doctor dropped some word, like corruption of the blood, scarlatina, or else – heaven help us – diphtheria, and off she went.

It was impossible for it to be otherwise. Women in the old days had the belief that 'God has given, God has taken away,' that the soul of the little angel is going to heaven, and that it is better to die innocent than to die in sin. If the women of to-day had something like this faith, they could endure more peacefully the sickness of their children. But of all that there does not remain even a trace. And yet it is necessary to believe in something; consequently they stupidly believe in medicine, and not even in medicine, but in the doctor. One believes in X, another in Z, and, like all believers, they do not see the idiocy of their beliefs. They believe quia absurdum, because, in reality, if they did not believe in a stupid way, they would see the vanity of all that these brigands prescribe for them. Scarlatina is a contagious disease; so, when one lives in a large city, half the family has to move away from its residence (we did it twice), and yet every man in the city is a centre through which pass innumerable diameters, carrying threads of all sorts of contagions. There is no obstacle: the baker, the tailor, the coachman, the laundresses.

"And I would undertake, for every man who moves on account of contagion, to find in his new dwelling-place another contagion similar, if not the same.

But that is not all. Every one knows rich people who, after a case of diphtheria, destroy everything in their residences, and then fall sick in houses newly built and furnished. Every one knows, likewise, numbers of men who come in contact with sick people and do not get infected. Our anxieties are due to the people who circulate tall stories. One woman says that she has an excellent doctor. 'Pardon me,' answers the other, 'he killed such a one,' or such a one. And vice versa. Bring her another, who knows no more, who learned from the same books, who treats according to the same formulas, but who goes about in a carriage, and asks a hundred roubles a visit, and she will have faith in him.

It all lies in the fact that our women are savages. They have no belief in God, but some of them believe in the evil eye, and the others in doctors who charge high fees. If they had faith they would know that scarlatina, diphtheria, etc., are not so terrible, since they cannot disturb that which man can and should love, – the soul. There can result from them only that which none of us can avoid, – disease and death. Without faith in God, they love only physically, and all their energy is concentrated upon the preservation of life, which cannot be preserved, and which the doctors promise the fools of both sexes to save. And from that time there is nothing to be done; the doctors must be summoned.

Thus the presence of the children not only did not improve our relations as husband and wife, but, on the contrary, disunited us. The children became an additional cause of dispute, and the larger they grew, the more they became an instrument of struggle.

"One would have said that we used them as weapons with which to combat each other. Each of us had his favorite. I made use of little Basile (the eldest), she of Lise. Further, when the children reached an age where their characters began to be defined, they became allies, which we drew each in his or her own direction. They suffered horribly from this, the poor things, but we, in our perpetual hubbub, were not clear-headed enough to think of them. The little girl was devoted to me, but the eldest boy, who resembled my wife, his favorite, often inspired me with dislike."

# CHAPTER XVII

We lived at first in the country, then in the city, and, if the final misfortune had not happened, I should have lived thus until my old age and should then have believed that I had had a good life, – not too good, but, on the other hand, not bad, – an existence such as other people lead. I should not have understood the abyss of misfortune and ignoble falsehood in which I floundered about, feeling that something was not right. I felt, in the first place, that I, a man, who, according to my ideas, ought to be the master, wore the petticoats, and that I could not get rid of them. The principal cause of my subjection was the children. I should have liked to free myself, but I could not. Bringing up the children, and resting upon them, my wife ruled. I did not then realize that she could not help ruling, especially because, in marrying, she was morally superior to me, as every young girl is incomparably superior to the man, since she is incomparably purer. Strange thing! The ordinary wife in our society is a very commonplace person or worse, selfish, gossiping, whimsical, whereas the ordinary young girl, until the age of twenty, is a charming being, ready for everything that is beautiful and lofty. Why is this so? Evidently because husbands pervert them, and lower them to their own level.

In truth, if boys and girls are born equal, the little girls find themselves in a better situation. In the first place, the young girl is not subjected to the perverting conditions to which we are subjected. She has neither cigarettes, nor wine, nor cards, nor comrades, nor public houses, nor public functions. And then the chief thing is that she is physically pure, and that is why, in marrying, she is superior to her husband. She is superior to man as a young girl, and when she becomes a wife in our society, where there is no need to work in order to live, she becomes superior, also, by the gravity of the acts of generation, birth, and nursing.

Woman, in bringing a child into the world, and giving it her bosom, sees clearly that her affair is more serious than the affair of man, who sits in the Zemstvo, in the court. She knows that in these functions the main thing is money, and money can be made in different ways, and for that very reason money is not inevitably necessary, like nursing a child. Consequently woman is necessarily superior to man, and must rule. But man, in our society, not only does not recognize this, but, on the contrary, always looks upon her from the height of his grandeur, despising what she does.

Thus my wife despised me for my work at the Zemstvo, because she gave birth to children and nursed them. I, in turn, thought that woman's labor was most contemptible, which one might and should laugh at.

Apart from the other motives, we were also separated by a mutual contempt. Our relations grew ever more hostile, and we arrived at that period when, not only did dissent provoke hostility, but hostility provoked dissent. Whatever she might say, I was sure in advance to hold a contrary opinion; and she the same. Toward the fourth year of our marriage it was tacitly decided between us that no intellectual community was possible, and we made no further attempts at it. As to the simplest objects, we each held obstinately to our own opinions. With strangers we talked upon the most varied and most intimate matters, but not with each other. Sometimes, in listening to my wife talk with others in my presence, I said to myself: 'What a woman! Everything that she says is a lie!' And I was astonished that the person with whom she was conversing did not see that she was lying. When we were together; we were condemned to silence, or to conversations which, I am sure, might have been carried on by animals.

'What time is it? It is bed-time. What is there for dinner to-day? Where shall we go? What is there in the newspaper? The doctor must be sent for, Lise has a sore throat.'

Unless we kept within the extremely narrow limits of such conversation, irritation was sure to ensue. The presence of a third person relieved us, for through an intermediary we could still communicate. She probably believed that she was always right. As for me, in my own eyes, I was a saint beside her.

The periods of what we call love arrived as often as formerly. They were more brutal, without refinement, without ornament; but they were short, and generally followed by periods of irritation without cause, irritation fed by the most trivial pretexts. We had spats about the coffee, the table-cloth, the carriage, games of cards, – trifles, in short, which could not be of the least importance to either of us. As for me, a terrible execration was continually boiling up within me. I watched her pour the tea, swing her foot, lift her spoon to her mouth, and blow upon hot liquids or sip them, and I detested her as if these had been so many crimes.

I did not notice that these periods of irritation depended very regularly upon the periods of love. Each of the latter was followed by one of the former. A period of intense love was followed by a long period of anger; a period of mild love induced a mild irritation. We did not understand that this love and this hatred were two opposite faces of the same animal feeling. To live thus would be terrible, if one understood the philosophy of it. But we did not perceive this, we did not analyze it. It is at once the torture and the relief of man that, when he lives irregularly, he can cherish illusions as to the miseries of his situation. So did we. She tried to forget herself in sudden and absorbing occupations, in household duties, the care of the furniture, her dress and that of her children, in the education of the latter, and in looking after their health. These were occupations that did not arise from any immediate necessity, but she accomplished them as if her life and that of her children depended on whether the pastry was allowed to burn, whether a curtain was hanging properly, whether a dress was a success, whether a lesson was well learned, or whether a medicine was swallowed.

I saw clearly that to her all this was, more than anything else, a means of forgetting, an intoxication, just as hunting, card-playing, and my functions at the Zemstvo served the same purpose for me. It is true that in addition I had an intoxication literally speaking, – tobacco, which I smoked in large quantities, and wine, upon which I did not get drunk, but of which I took too much. Vodka before meals, and during meals two glasses of wine, so that a perpetual mist concealed the turmoil of existence.

These new theories of hypnotism, of mental maladies, of hysteria are not simple stupidities, but dangerous or evil stupidities. Charcot, I am sure, would have said that my wife was hysterical, and of me he would have said that I was an abnormal being, and he would have wanted to treat me. But in us there was nothing requiring treatment. All this mental malady was the simple result of the fact that we were living immorally. Thanks to this immoral life, we suffered, and, to stifle our sufferings, we tried abnormal means, which the doctors call

the 'symptoms' of a mental malady, —
hysteria.

There was no occasion in all this to apply
for treatment to Charcot or to anybody
else. Neither suggestion nor bromide
would have been effective in working our
cure. The needful thing was an
examination of the origin of the evil. It
is as when one is sitting on a nail; if you
see the nail, you see that which is
irregular in your life, and you avoid it.
Then the pain stops, without any necessity
of stifling it. Our pain arose from the
irregularity of our life, and also my
jealousy, my irritability, and the necessity
of keeping myself in a state of perpetual
semi-intoxication by hunting, card-playing,
and, above all, the use of wine and
tobacco. It was because of this irregularity
that my wife so passionately pursued her
occupations. The sudden changes of her
disposition, from extreme sadness to
extreme gayety, and her babble, arose
from the need of forgetting herself, of
forgetting her life, in the continual
intoxication of varied and very brief
occupations.

"Thus we lived in a perpetual fog, in which we did not distinguish our condition. We were like two galley-slaves fastened to the same ball, cursing each other, poisoning each other's existence, and trying to shake each other off. I was still unaware that ninety-nine families out of every hundred live in the same hell, and that it cannot be otherwise. I had not learned this fact from others or from myself. The coincidences that are met in regular, and even in irregular life, are surprising. At the very period when the life of parents becomes impossible, it becomes indispensable that they go to the city to live, in order to educate their children. That is what we did."

Posdnicheff became silent, and twice there escaped him, in the half-darkness, sighs, which at that moment seemed to me like suppressed sobs. Then he continued.

# CHAPTER XVIII

So we lived in the city. In the city the wretched feel less sad. One can live there a hundred years without being noticed, and be dead a long time before anybody will notice it. People have no time to inquire into your life. All are absorbed. Business, social relations, art, the health of children, their education. And there are visits that must be received and made; it is necessary to see this one, it is necessary to hear that one or the other one. In the city there are always one, two, or three celebrities that it is indispensable that one should visit.

Now one must care for himself, or care for such or such a little one, now it is the professor, the private tutor, the governesses, . . . and life is absolutely empty. In this activity we were less conscious of the sufferings of our cohabitation. Moreover, in the first of it, we had a superb occupation, – the arrangement of the new dwelling, and then, too, the moving from the city to the country, and from the country to the city.

Thus we spent a winter. The following winter an incident happened to us which passed unnoticed, but which was the fundamental cause of all that happened later. My wife was suffering, and the rascals (the doctors) would not permit her to conceive a child, and taught her how to avoid it. I was profoundly disgusted. I struggled vainly against it, but she insisted frivolously and obstinately, and I surrendered. The last justification of our life as wretches was thereby suppressed, and life became baser than ever.

The peasant and the workingman need children, and hence their conjugal relations have a justification. But we, when we have a few children, have no need of any more. They make a superfluous confusion of expenses and joint heirs, and are an embarrassment. Consequently we have no excuses for our existence as wretches, but we are so deeply degraded that we do not see the necessity of a justification. The majority of people in contemporary society give themselves up to this debauchery without the slightest remorse. We have no conscience left, except, so to speak, the conscience of public opinion and of the criminal code. But in this matter neither of these consciences is struck. There is not a being in society who blushes at it. Each one practices it, – X, Y, Z, etc. What is the use of multiplying beggars, and depriving ourselves of the joys of social life? There is no necessity of having conscience before the criminal code, or of fearing it: low girls, soldiers' wives who throw their children into ponds or wells, these certainly must be put in prison. But with us the suppression is effected opportunely and properly.

"Thus we passed two years more. The method prescribed by the rascals had evidently succeeded. My wife had grown stouter and handsomer. It was the beauty of the end of summer. She felt it, and paid much attention to her person. She had acquired that provoking beauty that stirs men. She was in all the brilliancy of the wife of thirty years, who conceives no children, eats heartily, and is excited. The very sight of her was enough to frighten one. She was like a spirited carriage-horse that has long been idle, and suddenly finds itself without a bridle. As for my wife, she had no bridle, as for that matter, ninety-nine hundredths of our women have none."

# CHAPTER XIX

Posdnicheff's face had become trans-formed; his eyes were pitiable; their expression seemed strange, like that of another being than himself; his moustache and beard turned up toward the top of his face; his nose was diminished, and his mouth enlarged, immense, frightful.

"Yes," he resumed "she had grown stouter since ceasing to conceive, and her anxieties about her children began to disappear. Not even to disappear. One would have said that she was waking from a long intoxication, that on coming to herself she had perceived the entire universe with its joys, a whole world in which she had not learned to live, and which she did not understand."

'If only this world shall not vanish! When time is past, when old age comes, one cannot recover it.' Thus, I believe, she thought, or rather felt. Moreover, she could neither think nor feel otherwise. She had been brought up in this idea that there is in the world but one thing worthy of attention, – love. In marrying, she had known something of this love, but very far from everything that she had understood as promised her, everything that she expected. How many disillusions! How much suffering! And an unexpected torture, – the children! This torture had told upon her, and then, thanks to the obliging doctor, she had learned that it is possible to avoid having children. That had made her glad. She had tried, and she was now revived for the only thing that she knew, – for love. But love with a husband polluted by jealousy and ill-nature was no longer her ideal. She began to think of some other tenderness; at least, that is what I thought. She looked about her as if expecting some event or some being. I noticed it, and I could not help being anxious.

Always, now, it happened that, in talking with me through a third party (that is, in talking with others, but with the intention that I should hear), she boldly expressed, – not thinking that an hour before she had said the opposite, – half joking, half seriously, this idea that maternal anxieties are a delusion; that it is not worth while to sacrifice one's life to children. When one is young, it is necessary to enjoy life. So she occupied herself less with the children, not with the same intensity as formerly, and paid more and more attention to herself, to her face, – although she concealed it, – to her pleasures, and even to her perfection from the worldly point of view. She began to devote herself passionately to the piano, which had formerly stood forgotten in the corner. There, at the piano, began the adventure.

"The MAN appeared."

Posdnicheff seemed embarrassed, and twice again there escaped him that nasal sound of which I spoke above. I thought that it gave him pain to refer to the MAN, and to remember him. He made an effort, as if to break down the obstacle that embarrassed him, and continued with determination.

"He was a bad man in my eyes, and not because he has played such an important role in my life, but because he was really such. For the rest, from the fact that he was bad, we must conclude that he was irresponsible. He was a musician, a violinist. Not a professional musician, but half man of the world, half artist. His father, a country proprietor, was a neighbor of my father's. The father had become ruined, and the children, three boys, were all sent away. Our man, the youngest, was sent to his godmother at Paris. There they placed him in the Conservatory, for he showed a taste for music. He came out a violinist, and played in concerts."

On the point of speaking evil of the other, Posdnicheff checked himself, stopped, and said suddenly:

In truth, I know not how he lived. I only know that that year he came to Russia, and came to see me. Moist eyes of almond shape, smiling red lips, a little moustache well waxed, hair brushed in the latest fashion, a vulgarly pretty face, – what the women call 'not bad,' – feebly built physically, but with no deformity; with hips as broad as a woman's; correct, and insinuating himself into the familiarity of people as far as possible, but having that keen sense that quickly detects a false step and retires in reason, – a man, in short, observant of the external rules of dignity, with that special Parisianism that is revealed in buttoned boots, a gaudy cravat, and that something which foreigners pick up in Paris, and which, in its peculiarity and novelty, always has an influence on our women. In his manners an external and artificial gayety, a way, you know, of referring to everything by hints, by unfinished fragments, as if everything that one says you knew already, recalled it, and could supply the omissions. Well, he, with his music, was the cause of all.

"At the trial the affair was so represented that everything seemed attributable to jealousy. It is false, – that is, not quite false, but there was something else. The verdict was rendered that I was a deceived husband, that I had killed in defence of my sullied honor (that is the way they put it in their language), and thus I was acquitted. I tried to explain the affair from my own point of view, but they concluded that I simply wanted to rehabilitate the memory of my wife. Her relations with the musician, whatever they may have been, are now of no importance to me or to her. The important part is what I have told you. The whole tragedy was due to the fact that this man came into our house at a time when an immense abyss had already been dug between us, that frightful tension of mutual hatred, in which the slightest motive sufficed to precipitate the crisis. Our quarrels in the last days were something terrible, and the more astonishing because they were followed by a brutal passion extremely strained. If it had not been he, some other would have come. If the pretext had not been jealousy, I should have discovered another. I insist upon this point, – that all husbands who live the married life that I lived must either resort to outside debauchery, or separate from their wives, or kill themselves, or kill their wives as I did. If there is any one in my case to whom this does not happen, he is a very rare exception, for, before ending as I ended, I was several times on the point of suicide, and my wife made several attempts to poison herself."

# CHAPTER XX

In order that you may understand me, I must tell you how this happened. We were living along, and all seemed well. Suddenly we began to talk of the children's education. I do not remember what words either of us uttered, but a discussion began, reproaches, leaps from one subject to another. 'Yes, I know it. It has been so for a long time.' . . . 'You said that.' . . . 'No, I did not say that.' . . . 'Then I lie?' etc.

And I felt that the frightful crisis was approaching when I should desire to kill her or else myself. I knew that it was approaching; I was afraid of it as of fire; I wanted to restrain myself. But rage took possession of my whole being. My wife found herself in the same condition, perhaps worse. She knew that she intentionally distorted each of my words, and each of her words was saturated with venom. All that was dear to me she disparaged and profaned. The farther the quarrel went, the more furious it became. I cried, 'Be silent,' or something like that.

She bounded out of the room and ran toward the children. I tried to hold her back to finish my insults. I grasped her by the arm, and hurt her. She cried: 'Children, your father is beating me.' I cried: 'Don't lie.' She continued to utter falsehoods for the simple purpose of irritating me further. 'Ah, it is not the first time,' or something of that sort. The children rushed toward her and tried to quiet her. I said: 'Don't sham.' She said: 'You look upon everything as a sham. You would kill a person and say he was shamming. Now I understand you. That is what you want to do.' 'Oh, if you were only dead!' I cried.

I remember how that terrible phrase frightened me. Never had I thought that I could utter words so brutal, so frightful, and I was stupefied at what had just escaped my lips. I fled into my private apartment. I sat down and began to smoke. I heard her go into the hall and prepare to go out. I asked her:

'Where are you going? She did not answer. 'Well, may the devil take you!' said I to myself, going back into my private room, where I lay down again and began smoking afresh. Thousands of plans of vengeance, of ways of getting rid of her, and how to arrange this, and act as if nothing had happened, – all this passed through my head. I thought of these things, and I smoked, and smoked, and smoked. I thought of running away, of making my escape, of going to America. I went so far as to dream how beautiful it would be, after getting rid of her, to love another woman, entirely different from her. I should be rid of her if she should die or if I should get a divorce, and I tried to think how that could be managed. I saw that I was getting confused, but, in order not to see that I was not thinking rightly, I kept on smoking.

And the life of the house went on as usual. The children's teacher came and asked: 'Where is Madame? When will she return?'

The servants asked if they should serve the tea. I entered the dining-room. The children, Lise, the eldest girl, looked at me with fright, as if to question me, and she did not come. The whole evening passed, and still she did not come. Two sentiments kept succeeding each other in my soul, – hatred of her, since she tortured myself and the children by her absence, but would finally return just the same, and fear lest she might return and make some attempt upon herself. But where should I look for her? At her sister's? It seemed so stupid to go to ask where one's wife is. Moreover, may God forbid, I hoped, that she should be at her sister's! If she wishes to torment any one, let her torment herself first. And suppose she were not at her sister's.

"Suppose she were to do, or had already done, something.

Eleven o'clock, midnight, one o'clock . . . I did not sleep. I did not go to my chamber. It is stupid to lie stretched out all alone, and to wait. But in my study I did not rest. I tried to busy myself, to write letters, to read. Impossible! I was alone, tortured, wicked, and I listened. Toward daylight I went to sleep. I awoke. She had not returned. Everything in the house went on as usual, and all looked at me in astonishment, questioningly. The children's eyes were full of reproach for me.

And always the same feeling of anxiety about her, and of hatred because of this anxiety.

Toward eleven o'clock in the morning came her sister, her ambassadress. Then began the usual phrases: 'She is in a terrible state. What is the matter?' 'Why, nothing has happened.' I spoke of her asperity of character, and I added that I had done nothing, and that I would not take the first step. If she wants a divorce, so much the better! My sister-in-law would not listen to this idea, and went away without having gained anything. I was obstinate, and I said boldly and determinedly, in talking to her, that I would not take the first step. Immediately she had gone I went into the other room, and saw the children in a frightened and pitiful state, and there I found myself already inclined to take this first step. But I was bound by my word. Again I walked up and down, always smoking. At breakfast I drank brandy and wine, and I reached the point which I unconsciously desired, the point where I no longer saw the stupidity and baseness of my situation.

Toward three o'clock she came. I thought that she was appeased, or admitted her defeat. I began to tell her that I was provoked by her reproaches. She answered me, with the same severe and terribly downcast face, that she had not come for explanations, but to take the children, that we could not live together. I answered that it was not my fault, that she had put me beside myself. She looked at me with a severe and solemn air, and said: 'Say no more. You will repent it.' I said that I could not tolerate comedies. Then she cried out something that I did not understand, and rushed toward her room. The key turned in the lock, and she shut herself up. I pushed at the door. There was no response. Furious, I went away.

A half hour later Lise came running all in tears. 'What! Has anything happened? We cannot hear Mamma!' We went toward my wife's room. I pushed the door with all my might. The bolt was scarcely drawn, and the door opened. In a skirt, with high boots, my wife lay awkwardly on the bed. On the table an empty opium phial. We restored her to life. Tears and then reconciliation! Not reconciliation; internally each kept the hatred for the other, but it was absolutely necessary for the moment to end the scene in some way, and life began again as before. These scenes, and even worse, came now once a week, now every month, now every day. And invariably the same incidents. Once I was absolutely resolved to fly, but through some inconceivable weakness I remained.

"Such were the circumstances in which we were living when the MAN came. The man was bad, it is true. But what! No worse than we were."

# CHAPTER XXI

When we moved to Moscow, this gentleman – his name was Troukhatchevsky –
came to my house. It was in the morning.
I received him. In former times we had
been very familiar. He tried, by various
advances, to re-establish the familiarity,
but I was determined to keep him at a
distance, and soon he gave it up. He
displeased me extremely. At the first
glance I saw that he was a filthy
debauche. I was jealous of him, even
before he had seen my wife. But, strange
thing! some occult fatal power kept me
from repulsing him and sending him
away, and, on the contrary, induced me
to suffer this approach. What could have
been simpler than to talk with him a few
minutes, and then dismiss him coldly
without introducing him to my wife? But
no, as if on purpose, I turned the
conversation upon his skill as a violinist,
and he answered that, contrary to what
I had heard, he now played the violin
more than formerly. He remembered that
I used to play. I answered that I had

abandoned music, but that my wife played very well.

Singular thing! Why, in the important events of our life, in those in which a man's fate is decided, – as mine was decided in that moment, – why in these events is there neither a past nor a future? My relations with Troukhatchevsky the first day, at the first hour, were such as they might still have been after all that has happened. I was conscious that some frightful misfortune must result from the presence of this man, and, in spite of that, I could not help being amiable to him. I introduced him to my wife. She was pleased with him. In the beginning, I suppose, because of the pleasure of the violin playing, which she adored. She had even hired for that purpose a violinist from the theatre. But when she cast a glance at me, she understood my feelings, and concealed her impression. Then began the mutual trickery and deceit. I smiled agreeably, pretending that all this pleased me extremely. He, looking at my wife, as all debauches look at beautiful women, with an air of being interested solely in the subject of conversation, – that is, in that which did not interest him at all.

She tried to seem indifferent. But my expression, my jealous or false smile, which she knew so well, and the voluptuous glances of the musician, evidently excited her. I saw that, after the first interview, her eyes were already glittering, glittering strangely, and that, thanks to my jealousy, between him and her had been immediately established that sort of electric current which is provoked by an identity of expression in the smile and in the eyes.

We talked, at the first interview, of music, of Paris, and of all sorts of trivialities. He rose to go. Pressing his hat against his swaying hip, he stood erect, looking now at her and now at me, as if waiting to see what she would do. I remember that minute, precisely because it was in my power not to invite him. I need not have invited him, and then nothing would have happened. But I cast a glance first at him, then at her. 'Don't flatter yourself that I can be jealous of you,' I thought, addressing myself to her mentally, and I invited the other to bring his violin that very evening, and to play with my wife. She raised her eyes toward me with astonishment, and her face turned purple, as if she were seized with a sudden fear. She began to excuse herself, saying that she did not play well enough. This refusal only excited me the more. I remember the strange feeling with which I looked at his neck, his white neck, in contrast with his black hair, separated by a parting, when, with his skipping gait, like that of a bird, he left my house. I could not help confessing to myself that this man's presence caused me suffering. 'It is in my power,' thought I, 'to so arrange things that I shall never see him again. But can it be that I, I, fear him? No, I do not fear him. It would be too humiliating!'

And there in the hall, knowing that my wife heard me, I insisted that he should come that very evening with his violin. He promised me, and went away. In the evening he arrived with his violin, and they played together. But for a long time things did not go well; we had not the necessary music, and that which we had my wife could not play at sight. I amused myself with their difficulties. I aided them, I made proposals, and they finally executed a few pieces, – songs without words, and a little sonata by Mozart. He played in a marvellous manner. He had what is called the energetic and tender tone. As for difficulties, there were none for him. Scarcely had he begun to play, when his face changed. He became serious, and much more sympathetic. He was, it is needless to say, much stronger than my wife. He helped her, he advised her simply and naturally, and at the same time played his game with courtesy. My wife seemed interested only in the music. She was very simple and agreeable. Throughout the evening I feigned, not only for the others, but for myself, an interest solely in the music. Really, I was continually tortured by jealousy. From the first minute that the musician's eyes met those of my wife, I saw that he did not regard her as a disagreeable woman, with whom on occasion it would be unpleasant to enter into intimate relations.

If I had been pure, I should not have dreamed of what he might think of her. But I looked at women, and that is why I understood him and was in torture. I was in torture, especially because I was sure that toward me she had no other feeling than of perpetual irritation, sometimes interrupted by the customary sensuality, and that this man, – thanks to his external elegance and his novelty, and, above all, thanks to his unquestionably remarkable talent, thanks to the attraction exercised under the influence of music, thanks to the impression that music produces upon nervous natures, – this man would not only please, but would inevitably, and without difficulty, subjugate and conquer her, and do with her as he liked.

I could not help seeing this. I could not help suffering, or keep from being jealous. And I was jealous, and I suffered, and in spite of that, and perhaps even because of that, an unknown force, in spite of my will, impelled me to be not only polite, but more than polite, amiable. I cannot say whether I did it for my wife, or to show him that I did not fear HIM, or to deceive myself; but from my first relations with him I could not be at my ease. I was obliged, that I might not give way to a desire to kill him immediately, to 'caress' him. I filled his glass at the table, I grew enthusiastic over his playing, I talked to him with an extremely amiable smile, and I invited him to dinner the following Sunday, and to play again. I told him that I would invite some of my acquaintances, lovers of his art, to hear him.

Two or three days later I was entering my house, in conversation with a friend, when in the hall I suddenly felt something as heavy as a stone weighing on my heart, and I could not account for it. And it was this, it was this: in passing through the hall, I had noticed something which reminded me of HIM. Not until I reached my study did I realize what it was, and I returned to the hall to verify my conjecture. Yes, I was not mistaken. It was his overcoat (everything that belonged to him, I, without realizing it, had observed with extraordinary attention). I questioned the servant. That was it. He had come.

I passed near the parlor, through my children's study-room. Lise, my daughter, was sitting before a book, and the old nurse, with my youngest child, was beside the table, turning the cover of something or other. In the parlor I heard a slow arpeggio, and his voice, deadened, and a denial from her. She said: 'No, no! There is something else!' And it seemed to me that some one was purposely deadening the words by the aid of the piano.

My God! How my heart leaped! What were my imaginations! When I remember the beast that lived in me at that moment, I am seized with fright. My heart was first compressed, then stopped, and then began to beat like a hammer. The principal feeling, as in every bad feeling, was pity for myself. 'Before the children, before the old nurse,' thought I, 'she dishonors me. I will go away. I can endure it no longer. God knows what I should do if . . . But I must go in.'

The old nurse raised her eyes to mine, as if she understood, and advised me to keep a sharp watch. 'I must go in,' I said to myself, and, without knowing what I did, I opened the door. He was sitting at the piano and making arpeggios with his long, white, curved fingers. She was standing in the angle of the grand piano, before the open score. She saw or heard me first, and raised her eyes to mine. Was she stunned, was she pretending not to be frightened, or was she really not frightened at all? In any case, she did not tremble, she did not stir. She blushed, but only a little later.

'How glad I am that you have come! We have not decided what we will play Sunday,' said she, in a tone that she would not have had if she had been alone with me.

"This tone, and the way in which she said 'we' in speaking of herself and of him, revolted me. I saluted him silently. He shook hands with me directly, with a smile that seemed to me full of mockery. He explained to me that he had brought some scores, in order to prepare for the Sunday concert, and that they were not in accord as to the piece to choose, – whether difficult, classic things, notably a sonata by Beethoven, or lighter pieces.

And as he spoke, he looked at me. It was all so natural, so simple, that there was absolutely nothing to be said against it. And at the same time I saw, I was sure, that it was false, that they were in a conspiracy to deceive me.

One of the most torturing situations for the jealous (and in our social life everybody is jealous) are those social conditions which allow a very great and dangerous intimacy between a man and a woman under certain pretexts. One must make himself the laughing stock of everybody, if he desires to prevent associations in the ball-room, the intimacy of doctors with their patients, the familiarity of art occupations, and especially of music. In order that people may occupy themselves together with the noblest art, music, a certain intimacy is necessary, in which there is nothing blameworthy. Only a jealous fool of a husband can have anything to say against it. A husband should not have such thoughts, and especially should not thrust his nose into these affairs, or prevent them. And yet, everybody knows that precisely in these occupations, especially in music, many adulteries originate in our society.

"I had evidently embarrassed them, because for some time I was unable to say anything. I was like a bottle suddenly turned upside down, from which the water does not run because it is too full. I wanted to insult the man, and to drive him away, but I could do nothing of the kind. On the contrary, I felt that I was disturbing them, and that it was my fault. I made a presence of approving everything, this time also, thanks to that strange feeling that forced me to treat him the more amiably in proportion as his presence was more painful to me. I said that I trusted to his taste, and I advised my wife to do the same. He remained just as long as it was necessary in order to efface the unpleasant impression of my abrupt entrance with a frightened face. He went away with an air of satisfaction at the conclusions arrived at. As for me, I was perfectly sure that, in comparison with that which preoccupied them, the question of music was indifferent to them. I accompanied him with especial courtesy to the hall (how can one help accompanying a man who has come to disturb your tranquillity and ruin the happiness of the entire family?), and I shook his white, soft hand with fervent amiability."

# CHAPTER XXII

All that day I did not speak to my wife. I could not. Her proximity excited such hatred that I feared myself. At the table she asked me, in presence of the children, when I was to start upon a journey. I was to go the following week to an assembly of the Zemstvo, in a neighboring locality. I named the date. She asked me if I would need anything for the journey. I did not answer. I sat silent at the table, and silently I retired to my study. In those last days she never entered my study, especially at that hour. Suddenly I heard her steps, her walk, and then a terribly base idea entered my head that, like the wife of Uri, she wished to conceal a fault already committed, and that it was for this reason that she came to see me at this unseasonable hour. 'Is it possible,' thought I, 'that she is coming to see me?' On hearing her step as it approached: 'If it is to see me that she is coming, then I am right.'

An inexpressible hatred invaded my soul. The steps drew nearer, and nearer, and nearer yet. Would she pass by and go on to the other room? No, the hinges creaked, and at the door her tall, graceful, languid figure appeared. In her face, in her eyes, a timidity, an insinuating expression, which she tried to hide, but which I saw, and of which I understood the meaning. I came near suffocating, such were my efforts to hold my breath, and, continuing to look at her, I took my cigarette, and lighted it.

'What does this mean? One comes to talk with you, and you go to smoking.'

And she sat down beside me on the sofa, resting against my shoulder. I recoiled, that I might not touch her.

'I see that you are displeased with what I wish to play on Sunday,' said she.

'I am not at all displeased,' said I.

'Can I not see?'

'Well, I congratulate you on your clairvoyance. Only to you every baseness is agreeable, and I abhor it.'

'If you are going to swear like a trooper, I am going away.'

'Then go away. Only know that, if the honor of the family is nothing to you, to me it is dear. As for you, the devil take you!'

"'What! What is the matter?'

'Go away, in the name of God.'

"But she did not go away. Was she pretending not to understand, or did she really not understand what I meant? But she was offended and became angry.

'You have become absolutely impossible,' she began, or some such phrase as that regarding my character, trying, as usual, to give me as much pain as possible. 'After what you have done to my sister (she referred to an incident with her sister, in which, beside myself, I had uttered brutalities; she knew that that tortured me, and tried to touch me in that tender spot) nothing will astonish me.'

'Yes, offended, humiliated, and dishonored, and after that to hold me still responsible,' thought I, and suddenly a rage, such a hatred invaded me as I do not remember to have ever felt before. For the first time I desired to express this hatred physically. I leaped upon her, but at the same moment I understood my condition, and I asked myself whether it would be well for me to abandon myself to my fury. And I answered myself that it would be well, that it would frighten her, and, instead of resisting, I lashed and spurred myself on, and was glad to feel my anger boiling more and more fiercely.

'Go away, or I will kill you!' I cried, purposely, with a frightful voice, and I grasped her by the arm. She did not go away. Then I twisted her arm, and pushed her away violently.

"'What is the matter with you? Come to your senses!' she shrieked.

'Go away,' roared I, louder than ever, rolling my eyes wildly. 'It takes you to put me in such a fury. I do not answer for myself! Go away!'

In abandoning myself to my anger, I became steeped in it, and I wanted to commit some violent act to show the force of my fury. I felt a terrible desire to beat her, to kill her, but I realized that that could not be, and I restrained myself. I drew back from her, rushed to the table, grasped the paper-weight, and threw it on the floor by her side. I took care to aim a little to one side, and, before she disappeared (I did it so that she could see it), I grasped a candlestick, which I also hurled, and then took down the barometer, continuing to shout:

'Go away! I do not answer for myself!'

She disappeared, and I immediately ceased my demonstrations. An hour later the old servant came to me and said that my wife was in a fit of hysterics. I went to see her. She sobbed and laughed, incapable of expressing anything, her whole body in a tremble. She was not shamming, she was really sick. We sent for the doctor, and all night long I cared for her. Toward daylight she grew calmer, and we became reconciled under the influence of that feeling which we called 'love.' The next morning, when, after the reconciliation, I confessed to her that I was jealous of Troukhatchevsky, she was not at all embarrassed, and began to laugh in the most natural way, so strange did the possibility of being led astray by such a man appear to her.

'With such a man can an honest woman entertain any feeling beyond the pleasure of enjoying music with him? But if you like, I am ready to never see him again, even on Sunday, although everybody has been invited. Write him that I am indisposed, and that will end the matter. Only one thing annoys me, – that any one could have thought him dangerous. I am too proud not to detest such thoughts.'

"And she did not lie. She believed what she said. She hoped by her words to provoke in herself a contempt for him, and thereby to defend herself. But she did not succeed. Everything was directed against her, especially that abominable music. So ended the quarrel, and on Sunday our guests came, and Troukhatchevsky and my wife again played together."

# CHAPTER XXIII

I think that it is superfluous to say that I was very vain. If one has no vanity in this life of ours, there is no sufficient reason for living. So for that Sunday I had busied myself in tastefully arranging things for the dinner and the musical soiree. I had purchased myself numerous things for the dinner, and had chosen the guests. Toward six o'clock they arrived, and after them Troukhatchevsky, in his dress-coat, with diamond shirt-studs, in bad taste. He bore himself with ease. To all questions he responded promptly, with a smile of contentment and understanding, and that peculiar expression which was intended to mean: 'All that you may do and say will be exactly what I expected.' Everything about him that was not correct I now noticed with especial pleasure, for it all tended to tranquillize me, and prove to me that to my wife he stood in such a degree of inferiority that, as she had told me, she could not stoop to his level. Less because of my wife's assurances than because of the atrocious sufferings which I felt in jealousy, I no longer allowed myself to be jealous.

"In spite of that, I was not at ease with the musician or with her during dinner-time and the time that elapsed before the beginning of the music. Involuntarily I followed each of their gestures and looks. The dinner, like all dinners, was tiresome and conventional. Not long afterward the music began. He went to get his violin; my wife advanced to the piano, and rummaged among the scores. Oh, how well I remember all the details of that evening! I remember how he brought the violin, how he opened the box, took off the serge embroidered by a lady's hand, and began to tune the instrument. I can still see my wife sit down, with a false air of indifference, under which it was plain that she hid a great timidity, a timidity that was especially due to her comparative lack of musical knowledge. She sat down with that false air in front of the piano, and then began the usual preliminaries, – the pizzicati of the violin and the arrangement of the scores. I remember then how they looked at each other, and cast a glance at their auditors who were taking their seats. They said a few words to each other, and the music began. They played Beethoven's 'Kreutzer Sonata.' Do you know the first presto? Do you know it? Ah!..."

Posdnicheff heaved a sigh, and was silent for a long time.

A terrible thing is that sonata, especially the presto! And a terrible thing is music in general. What is it? Why does it do what it does? They say that music stirs the soul. Stupidity! A lie! It acts, it acts frightfully (I speak for myself), but not in an ennobling way. It acts neither in an ennobling nor a debasing way, but in an irritating way. How shall I say it? Music makes me forget my real situation. It transports me into a state which is not my own. Under the influence of music I really seem to feel what I do not feel, to understand what I do not understand, to have powers which I cannot have. Music seems to me to act like yawning or laughter; I have no desire to sleep, but I yawn when I see others yawn; with no reason to laugh, I laugh when I hear others laugh. And music transports me immediately into the condition of soul in which he who wrote the music found himself at that time. I become confounded with his soul, and with him I pass from one condition to another. But why that? I know nothing about it? But he who wrote Beethoven's 'Kreutzer Sonata' knew well why he found himself in a certain condition. That condition led him to certain actions, and for that reason to him had a meaning, but to me none, none whatever. And that is why music provokes an excitement which it does not bring to a conclusion. For instance, a military march is played; the soldier passes to the sound of this march, and the music is finished. A dance is played; I have finished dancing, and the music is finished. A mass is sung; I receive the sacrament, and again the music is finished. But any other music provokes an excitement, and this excitement is not accompanied by the thing that needs properly to be done, and that is why music is so dangerous, and sometimes acts so frightfully.

In China music is under the control of the State, and that is the way it ought to be. Is it admissible that the first comer should hypnotize one or more persons, and then do with them as he likes? And especially that the hypnotizer should be the first immoral individual who happens to come along? It is a frightful power in the hands of any one, no matter whom. For instance, should they be allowed to play this 'Kreutzer Sonata,' the first presto, – and there are many like it, – in parlors, among ladies wearing low necked dresses, or in concerts, then finish the piece, receive the applause, and then begin another piece? These things should be played under certain circumstances, only in cases where it is necessary to incite certain actions corresponding to the music. But to incite an energy of feeling which corresponds to neither the time nor the place, and is expended in nothing, cannot fail to act dangerously. On me in particular this piece acted in a frightful manner. One would have said that new sentiments, new virtualities, of which I was formerly ignorant, had developed in me. 'Ah, yes, that's it! Not at all as I lived and thought before! This is the right way to live!'

Thus I spoke to my soul as I listened to that music. What was this new thing that I thus learned? That I did not realize, but the consciousness of this indefinite state filled me with joy. In that state there was no room for jealousy. The same faces, and among them HE and my wife, I saw in a different light. This music transported me into an unknown world, where there was no room for jealousy. Jealousy and the feelings that provoke it seemed to me trivialities, nor worth thinking of.

After the presto followed the andante, not very new, with commonplace variations, and the feeble finale. Then they played more, at the request of the guests, – first an elegy by Ernst, and then various other pieces. They were all very well, but did not produce upon me a tenth part of the impression that the opening piece did. I felt light and gay throughout the evening. As for my wife, never had I seen her as she was that night. Those brilliant eyes, that severity and majestic expression while she was playing, and then that utter languor, that weak, pitiable, and happy smile after she had finished, – I saw them all and attached no importance to them, believing that she felt as I did, that to her, as to me, new sentiments had been revealed, as through a fog. During almost the whole evening I was not jealous.

"Two days later I was to start for the assembly of the Zemstvo, and for that reason, on taking leave of me and carrying all his scores with him, Troukhatchevsky asked me when I should return. I inferred from that that he believed it impossible to come to my house during my absence, and that was agreeable to me. Now I was not to return before his departure from the city. So we bade each other a definite farewell. For the first time I shook his hand with pleasure, and thanked him for the satisfaction that he had given me. He likewise took leave of my wife, and their parting seemed to me very natural and proper. All went marvellously. My wife and I retired, well satisfied with the evening. We talked of our impressions in a general way, and we were nearer together and more friendly than we had been for a long time."

# CHAPTER XXIV

Two days later I started for the assembly, having bid farewell to my wife in an excellent and tranquil state of mind. In the district there was always much to be done. It was a world and a life apart. During two days I spent ten hours at the sessions. The evening of the second day, on returning to my district lodgings, I found a letter from my wife, telling me of the children, of their uncle, of the servants, and, among other things, as if it were perfectly natural, that Troukhatchevsky had been at the house, and had brought her the promised scores. He had also proposed that they play again, but she had refused.

For my part, I did not remember at all that he had promised any score. It had seemed to me on Sunday evening that he took a definite leave, and for this reason the news gave me a disagreeable surprise. I read the letter again. There was something tender and timid about it. It produced an extremely painful impression upon me. My heart swelled, and the mad beast of jealousy began to roar in his lair, and seemed to want to leap upon his prey. But I was afraid of this beast, and I imposed silence upon it.

What an abominable sentiment is jealousy! 'What could be more natural than what she has written?' said I to myself. I went to bed, thinking myself tranquil again. I thought of the business that remained to be done, and I went to sleep without thinking of her.

During these assemblies of the Zemstvo I always slept badly in my strange quarters. That night I went to sleep directly, but, as sometimes happens, a sort of sudden shock awoke me. I thought immediately of her, of my physical love for her, of Troukhatchevsky, and that between them everything had happened. And a feeling of rage compressed my heart, and I tried to quiet myself.

'How stupid!' said I to myself; 'there is no reason, none at all. And why humiliate ourselves, herself and myself, and especially myself, by supposing such horrors? This mercenary violinist, known as a bad man, – shall I think of him in connection with a respectable woman, the mother of a family, MY wife? How silly!' But on the other hand, I said to myself: 'Why should it not happen?'

Why? Was it not the same simple and intelligible feeling in the name of which I married, in the name of which I was living with her, the only thing I wanted of her, and that which, consequently, others desired, this musician among the rest? He was not married, was in good health (I remember how his teeth ground the gristle of the cutlets, and how eagerly he emptied the glass of wine with his red lips), was careful of his person, well fed, and not only without principles, but evidently with the principle that one should take advantage of the pleasure that offers itself. There was a bond between them, music, – the most refined form of sensual voluptuousness. What was there to restrain them? Nothing. Everything, on the contrary, attracted them. And she, she had been and had remained a mystery. I did not know her. I knew her only as an animal, and an animal nothing can or should restrain. And now I remember their faces on Sunday evening, when, after the 'Kreutzer Sonata,' they played a passionate piece, written I know not by whom, but a piece passionate to the point of obscenity.

'How could I have gone away?' said I to myself, as I recalled their faces. 'Was it not clear that between them everything was done that evening? Was it not clear that between them not only there were no more obstacles, but that both – especially she – felt a certain shame after what had happened at the piano? How weakly, pitiably, happily she smiled, as she wiped the perspiration from her reddened face! They already avoided each other's eyes, and only at the supper, when she poured some water for him, did they look at each other and smile imperceptibly.'

Now I remember with fright that look and that scarcely perceptible smile. 'Yes, everything has happened,' a voice said to me, and directly another said the opposite. 'Are you mad? It is impossible!' said the second voice.

"It was too painful to me to remain thus stretched in the darkness. I struck a match, and the little yellow-papered room frightened me. I lighted a cigarette, and, as always happens, when one turns in a circle of inextricable contradiction, I began to smoke. I smoked cigarette after cigarette to dull my senses, that I might not see my contradictions. All night I did not sleep, and at five o'clock, when it was not yet light, I decided that I could stand this strain no longer, and that I would leave directly. There was a train at eight o'clock. I awakened the keeper who was acting as my servant, and sent him to look for horses. To the assembly of Zemstvo I sent a message that I was called back to Moscow by pressing business, and that I begged them to substitute for me a member of the Committee. At eight o'clock I got into a tarantass and started off."

# CHAPTER XXV

I had to go twenty-five versts by carriage and eight hours by train. By carriage it was a very pleasant journey. The coolness of autumn was accompanied by a brilliant sun. You know the weather when the wheels imprint themselves upon the dirty road. The road was level, and the light strong, and the air strengthening. The tarantass was comfortable. As I looked at the horses, the fields, and the people whom we passed, I forgot where I was going. Sometimes it seemed to me that I was travelling without an object, – simply promenading, – and that I should go on thus to the end of the world. And I was happy when I so forgot myself. But when I remembered where I was going, I said to myself: 'I shall see later. Don't think about it.'

When half way, an incident happened to distract me still further. The tarantass, though new, broke down, and had to be repaired. The delays in looking for a telegue, the repairs, the payment, the tea in the inn, the conversation with the dvornik, all served to amuse me. Toward nightfall all was ready, and I started off again. By night the journey was still pleasanter than by day. The moon in its first quarter, a slight frost, the road still in good condition, the horses, the sprightly coachman, all served to put me in good spirits. I scarcely thought of what awaited me, and was gay perhaps because of the very thing that awaited me, and because I was about to say farewell to the joys of life.

But this tranquil state, the power of conquering my preoccupation, all ended with the carriage drive. Scarcely had I entered the cars, when the other thing began. Those eight hours on the rail were so terrible to me that I shall never forget them in my life. Was it because on entering the car I had a vivid imagination of having already arrived, or because the railway acts upon people in such an exciting fashion? At any rate, after boarding the train I could no longer control my imagination, which incessantly, with extraordinary vivacity, drew pictures before my eyes, each more cynical than its predecessor, which kindled my jealousy. And always the same things about what was happening at home during my absence. I burned with indignation, with rage, and with a peculiar feeling which steeped me in humiliation, as I contemplated these pictures. And I could not tear myself out of this condition. I could not help looking at them, I could not efface them, I could not keep from evoking them.

The more I looked at these imaginary pictures, the more I believed in their reality, forgetting that they had no serious foundation. The vivacity of these images seemed to prove to me that my imaginations were a reality. One would have said that a demon, against my will, was inventing and breathing into me the most terrible fictions. A conversation which dated a long time back, with the brother of Troukhatchevsky, I remembered at that moment, in a sort of ecstasy, and it tore my heart as I connected it with the musician and my wife. Yes, it was very long ago. The brother of Troukhatchevsky, answering my questions as to whether he frequented disreputable houses, said that a respectable man does not go where he may contract a disease, in a low and unclean spot, when one can find an honest woman. And here he, his brother, the musician, had found the honest woman. 'It is true that she is no longer in her early youth. She has lost a tooth on one side, and her face is slightly bloated,' thought I for Troukhatchevsky. 'But what is to be done? One must profit by what one has.'

'Yes, he is bound to take her for his mistress,' said I to myself again; 'and besides, she is not dangerous.'

'No, it is not possible' I rejoined in fright. 'Nothing, nothing of the kind has happened, and there is no reason to suppose there has. Did she not tell me that the very idea that I could be jealous of her because of him was humiliating to her?' 'Yes, but she lied,' I cried, and all began over again.

"There were only two travellers in my compartment: an old woman with her husband, neither of them very talkative; and even they got out at one of the stations, leaving me all alone. I was like a beast in a cage. Now I jumped up and approached the window, now I began to walk back and forth, staggering as if I hoped to make the train go faster by my efforts, and the car with its seats and its windows trembled continually, as ours does now."

And Posdnicheff rose abruptly, took a few steps, and sat down again.

Oh, I am afraid, I am afraid of railway carriages. Fear seizes me. I sat down again, and I said to myself: 'I must think of something else. For instance, of the inn keeper at whose house I took tea.' And then, in my imagination arose the dvornik, with his long beard, and his grandson, a little fellow of the same age as my little Basile. My little Basile! My little Basile! He will see the musician kiss his mother! What thoughts will pass through his poor soul! But what does that matter to her! She loves.

And again it all began, the circle of the same thoughts. I suffered so much that at last I did not know what to do with myself, and an idea passed through my head that pleased me much, – to get out upon the rails, throw myself under the cars, and thus finish everything. One thing prevented me from doing so. It was pity! It was pity for myself, evoking at the same time a hatred for her, for him, but not so much for him. Toward him I felt a strange sentiment of my humiliation and his victory, but toward her a terrible hatred.

'But I cannot kill myself and leave her free. She must suffer, she must understand at least that I have suffered,' said I to myself.

"At a station I saw people drinking at the lunch counter, and directly I went to swallow a glass of vodki. Beside me stood a Jew, drinking also. He began to talk to me, and I, in order not to be left alone in my compartment, went with him into his third-class, dirty, full of smoke, and covered with peelings and sunflower seeds. There I sat down beside the Jew, and, as it seemed, he told many anecdotes.

First I listened to him, but I did not understand what he said. He noticed it, and exacted my attention to his person. Then I rose and entered my own compartment.

'I must consider,' said I to myself, 'whether what I think is true, whether there is any reason to torment myself.' I sat down, wishing to reflect quietly; but directly, instead of the peaceful reflections, the same thing began again. Instead of the reasoning, the pictures.

'How many times have I tormented myself in this way,' I thought (I recalled previous and similar fits of jealousy), 'and then seen it end in nothing at all? It is the same now. Perhaps, yes, surely, I shall find her quietly sleeping. She will awaken, she will be glad, and in her words and looks I shall see that nothing has happened, that all this is vain. Ah, if it would only so turn out!' 'But no, that has happened too often! Now the end has come,' a voice said to me.

And again it all began. Ah, what torture! It is not to a hospital filled with syphilitic patients that I would take a young man to deprive him of the desire for women, but into my soul, to show him the demon which tore it. The frightful part was that I recognized in myself an indisputable right to the body of my wife, as if her body were entirely mine. And at the same time I felt that I could not possess this body, that it was not mine, that she could do with it as she liked, and that she liked to do with it as I did not like. And I was powerless against him and against her. He, like the Vanka of the song, would sing, before mounting the gallows, how he would kiss her sweet lips, etc., and he would even have the best of it before death. With her it was still worse. If she HAD NOT DONE IT, she had the desire, she wished to do it, and I knew that she did. That was worse yet. It would be better if she had already done it, to relieve me of my uncertainty.

"In short, I could not say what I desired. I desired that she might not want what she MUST want. It was complete madness."

# CHAPTER XXVI

At the station before the last, when the conductor came to take the tickets, I took my baggage and went out on the car platform, and the consciousness that the climax was near at hand only added to my agitation. I was cold, my jaw trembled so that my teeth chattered. Mechanically I left the station with the crowd, I took a tchik, and I started. I looked at the few people passing in the streets and at the dvorniks. I read the signs, without thinking of anything. After going half a verst my feet began to feel cold, and I remembered that in the car I had taken off my woollen socks, and had put them in my travelling bag. Where had I put the bag? Was it with me? Yes, and the basket?

I bethought myself that I had totally forgotten my baggage. I took out my check, and then decided it was not worth while to return. I continued on my way. In spite of all my efforts to remember, I cannot at this moment make out why I was in such a hurry. I know only that I was conscious that a serious and menacing event was approaching in my life. It was a case of real auto-suggestion. Was it so serious because I thought it so? Or had I a presentiment? I do not know. Perhaps, too, after what has happened, all previous events have taken on a lugubrious tint in my memory.

I arrived at the steps. It was an hour past midnight. A few isvotchiks were before the door, awaiting customers, attracted by the lighted windows (the lighted windows were those of our parlor and reception room). Without trying to account for this late illumination, I went up the steps, always with the same expectation of something terrible, and I rang. The servant, a good, industrious, and very stupid being, named Gregor, opened the door. The first thing that leaped to my eyes in the hall, on the hat-stand, among other garments, was an overcoat. I ought to have been astonished, but I was not astonished. I expected it. 'That's it!' I said to myself.

When I had asked Gregor who was there, and he had named Troukhatchevsky, I inquired whether there were other visitors. He answered: 'Nobody.' I remember the air with which he said that, with a tone that was intended to give me pleasure, and dissipate my doubts. 'That's it! that's it!' I had the air of saying to myself. 'And the children?'

"'Thank God, they are very well. They went to sleep long ago.'

I scarcely breathed, and I could not keep my jaw from trembling.

Then it was not as I thought. I had often before returned home with the thought that a misfortune had awaited me, but had been mistaken, and everything was going on as usual. But now things were not going on as usual. All that I had imagined, all that I believed to be chimeras, all really existed. Here was the truth.

I was on the point of sobbing, but straightway the demon whispered in my ear: 'Weep and be sentimental, and they will separate quietly, and there will be no proofs, and all your life you will doubt and suffer.' And pity for myself vanished, and there remained only the bestial need of some adroit, cunning, and energetic action. I became a beast, an intelligent beast.

'No, no,' said I to Gregor, who was about to announce my arrival. 'Do this, take a carriage, and go at once for my baggage. Here is the check. Start.'

He went along the hall to get his overcoat. Fearing lest he might frighten them, I accompanied him to his little room, and waited for him to put on his things. In the dining-room could be heard the sound of conversation and the rattling of knives and plates. They were eating. They had not heard the ring. 'Now if they only do not go out,' I thought.

Gregor put on his fur-collared coat and went out. I closed the door after him. I felt anxious when I was alone, thinking that directly I should have to act. How? I did not yet know. I knew only that all was ended, that there could be no doubt of his innocence, and that in an instant my relations with her were going to be terminated. Before, I had still doubts. I said to myself: 'Perhaps this is not true. Perhaps I am mistaken.' Now all doubt had disappeared. All was decided irrevocably. Secretly, all alone with him, at night! It is a violation of all duties! Or, worse yet, she may make a show of that audacity, of that insolence in crime, which, by its excess, tends to prove innocence. All is clear. No doubt. I feared but one thing, – that they might run in different directions, that they might invent some new lie, and thus deprive me of material proof, and of the sorrowful joy of punishing, yes, of executing them.

And to surprise them more quickly, I started on tiptoe for the dining-room, not through the parlor, but through the hall and the children's rooms. In the first room slept the little boy. In the second, the old nurse moved in her bed, and seemed on the point of waking, and I wondered what she would think when she knew all. And pity for myself gave me such a pang that I could not keep the tears back. Not to wake the children, I ran lightly through the hall into my study. I dropped upon the sofa, and sobbed. 'I, an honest man, I, the son of my parents, who all my life long have dreamed of family happiness, I who have never betrayed! . . . And here my five children, and she embracing a musician because he has red lips! No, she is not a woman! She is a bitch, a dirty bitch! Beside the chamber of the children, whom she had pretended to love all her life! And then to think of what she wrote me! And how do I know? Perhaps it has always been thus. Perhaps all these children, supposed to be mine, are the children of my servants. And if I had arrived to-morrow, she would have come to meet me with her coiffure, with her corsage, her indolent and graceful movements (and I see her attractive and ignoble features), and this jealous animal would have remained forever in my heart, tearing it. What will the old nurse say? And Gregor? And the poor little Lise? She already understands things. And this impudence, this falsehood, this bestial sensuality, that I know so well,' I said to myself.

I tried to rise. I could not. My heart was beating so violently that I could not hold myself upon my legs. 'Yes, I shall die of a rush of blood. She will kill me. That is what she wants. What is it to her to kill? But that would be too agreeable to him, and I will not allow him to have this pleasure.

Yes, here I am, and there they are. They are laughing, they . . . Yes, in spite of the fact that she is no longer in her early youth, he has not disdained her. At any rate, she is by no means ugly, and above all, not dangerous to his dear health, to him. Why did I not stifle her then?' said I to myself, as I remembered that other scene of the previous week, when I drove her from my study, and broke the furniture.

And I recalled the state in which I was then. Not only did I recall it, but I again entered into the same bestial state. And suddenly there came to me a desire to act, and all reasoning, except such as was necessary to action, vanished from my brain, and I was in the condition of a beast, and of a man under the influence of physical excitement pending a danger, who acts imperturbably, without haste, and yet without losing a minute, pursuing a definite object.

The first thing that I did was to take off my boots, and now, having only stockings on, I advanced toward the wall, over the sofa, where firearms and daggers were hanging, and I took down a curved Damascus blade, which I had never used, and which was very sharp. I took it from its sheath. I remember that the sheath fell upon the sofa, and that I said to myself: 'I must look for it later; it must not be lost.'

"Then I took off my overcoat, which I had kept on all the time, and with wolf-like tread started for THE ROOM. I do not remember how I proceeded, whether I ran or went slowly, through what chambers I passed, how I approached the dining-room, how I opened the door, how I entered. I remember nothing about it."

# CHAPTER XXVII

I Remember only the expression of their faces when I opened the door. I remember that, because it awakened in me a feeling of sorrowful joy. It was an expression of terror, such as I desired. Never shall I forget that desperate and sudden fright that appeared on their faces when they saw me. He, I believe, was at the table, and, when he saw or heard me, he started, jumped to his feet, and retreated to the sideboard. Fear was the only sentiment that could be read with certainty in his face. In hers, too, fear was to be read, but accompanied by other impressions. And yet, if her face had expressed only fear, perhaps that which happened would not have happened. But in the expression of her face there was at the first moment – at least, I thought I saw it – a feeling of ennui, of discontent, at this disturbance of her love and happiness. One would have said that her sole desire was not to be disturbed IN THE MOMENT OF HER HAPPINESS. But these expressions appeared upon their faces only for a moment. Terror almost immediately gave place to interrogation. Would they lie or not? If yes, they must begin. If not, something else was going to happen. But what?

He gave her a questioning glance. On her face the expression of anguish and ennui changed, it seemed to me, when she looked at him, into an expression of anxiety for HIM. For a moment I stood in the doorway, holding the dagger hidden behind my back. Suddenly he smiled, and in a voice that was indifferent almost to the point of ridicule, he said:

'We were having some music.'

'I did not expect –,' she began at the same time, chiming in with the tone of the other.

But neither he nor she finished their remarks. The same rage that I had felt the previous week took possession of me. I felt the need of giving free course to my violence and 'the joy of wrath.'

No, they did not finish. That other thing was going to begin, of which he was afraid, and was going to annihilate what they wanted to say. I threw myself upon her, still hiding the dagger, that he might not prevent me from striking where I desired, in her bosom, under the breast. At that moment he saw . . . and, what I did not expect on his part, he quickly seized my hand, and cried:

'Come to your senses! What are you doing? Help! Help!'

"I tore my hands from his grasp, and leaped upon him. I must have been very terrible, for he turned as white as a sheet, to his lips. His eyes scintillated singularly, and – again what I did not expect of him – he scrambled under the piano, toward the other room. I tried to follow him, but a very heavy weight fell upon my left arm. It was she.

I made an effort to clear myself. She clung more heavily than ever, refusing to let go. This unexpected obstacle, this burden, and this repugnant touch only irritated me the more. I perceived that I was completely mad, that I must be frightful, and I was glad of it. With a sudden impulse, and with all my strength, I dealt her, with my left elbow, a blow squarely in the face.

She uttered a cry and let go my arm. I wanted to follow the other, but I felt that it would be ridiculous to pursue in my stockings the lover of my wife, and I did not wish to be grotesque, I wished to be terrible. In spite of my extreme rage, I was all the time conscious of the impression that I was making upon others, and even this impression partially guided me.

I turned toward her. She had fallen on the long easy chair, and, covering her face at the spot where I had struck her, she looked at me. Her features exhibited fear and hatred toward me, her enemy, such as the rat exhibits when one lifts the rat-trap. At least, I saw nothing in her but that fear and hatred, the fear and hatred which love for another had provoked. Perhaps I still should have restrained myself, and should not have gone to the last extremity, if she had maintained silence. But suddenly she began to speak; she grasped my hand that held the dagger.

'Come to your senses! What are you doing? What is the matter with you? Nothing has happened, nothing, nothing! I swear it to you!'

I might have delayed longer, but these last words, from which I inferred the contrary of what they affirmed, – that is, that EVERYTHING had happened, – these words called for a reply. And the reply must correspond to the condition into which I had lashed myself, and which was increasing and must continue to increase. Rage has its laws.

'Do not lie, wretch. Do not lie!' I roared.

With my left hand I seized her hands. She disengaged herself. Then, without dropping my dagger, I seized her by the throat, forced her to the floor, and began to strangle her. With her two hands she clutched mine, tearing them from her throat, stifling. Then I struck her a blow with the dagger, in the left side, between the lower ribs.

When people say that they do not remember what they do in a fit of fury, they talk nonsense. It is false. I remember everything.

I did not lose my consciousness for a single moment. The more I lashed myself to fury, the clearer my mind became, and I could not help seeing what I did. I cannot say that I knew in advance what I would do, but at the moment when I acted, and it seems to me even a little before, I knew what I was doing, as if to make it possible to repent, and to be able to say later that I could have stopped.

I knew that I struck the blow between the ribs, and that the dagger entered.

At the second when I did it, I knew that I was performing a horrible act, such as I had never performed, − an act that would have frightful consequences. My thought was as quick as lightning, and the deed followed immediately. The act, to my inner sense, had an extraordinary clearness. I perceived the resistance of the corset and then something else, and then the sinking of the knife into a soft substance. She clutched at the dagger with her hands, and cut herself with it, but could not restrain the blow.

Long afterward, in prison when the moral revolution had been effected within me, I thought of that minute, I remembered it as far as I could, and I co-ordinated all the sudden changes. I remembered the terrible consciousness which I felt, – that I was killing a wife, MY wife.

I well remember the horror of that consciousness and I know vaguely that, having plunged in the dagger, I drew it out again immediately, wishing to repair and arrest my action. She straightened up and cried:

'Nurse, he has killed me!'

The old nurse, who had heard the noise, was standing in the doorway. I was still erect, waiting, and not believing myself in what had happened. But at that moment, from under her corset, the blood gushed forth. Then only did I understand that all reparation was impossible, and promptly I decided that it was not even necessary, that all had happened in accordance with my wish, and that I had fulfilled my desire. I waited until she fell, and until the nurse, exclaiming, 'Oh, my God!' ran to her; then only I threw away the dagger and went out of the room.

'I must not be agitated. I must be conscious of what I am doing,' I said to myself, looking neither at her nor at the old nurse. The latter cried and called the maid. I passed through the hall, and, after having sent the maid, started for my study.

'What shall I do now?' I asked myself.

And immediately I understood what I should do. Directly after entering the study, I went straight to the wall, took down the revolver, and examined it attentively. It was loaded. Then I placed it on the table. Next I picked up the sheath of the dagger, which had dropped down behind the sofa, and then I sat down. I remained thus for a long time. I thought of nothing, I did not try to remember anything. I heard a stifled noise of steps, a movement of objects and of tapestries, then the arrival of a person, and then the arrival of another person. Then I saw Gregor bring into my room the baggage from the railway; as if any one needed it!

"'Have you heard what has happened?' I asked him. 'Have you told the dvornik to inform the police?'

He made no answer, and went out. I rose, closed the door, took the cigarettes and the matches, and began to smoke. I had not finished one cigarette, when a drowsy feeling came over me and sent me into a deep sleep. I surely slept two hours. I remember having dreamed that I was on good terms with her, that after a quarrel we were in the act of making up, that something prevented us, but that we were friends all the same.

A knock at the door awoke me.

'It is the police,' thought I, as I opened my eyes. 'I have killed, I believe. But perhaps it is SHE; perhaps nothing has happened.'

Another knock. I did not answer. I was solving the question: 'Has it happened or not? Yes, it has happened.'

"I remembered the resistance of the corset, and then . . . 'Yes, it has happened. Yes, it has happened. Yes, now I must execute myself,' said I to myself.

I said it, but I knew well that I should not kill myself. Nevertheless, I rose and took the revolver, but, strange thing, I remembered that formerly I had very often had suicidal ideas, that that very night, on the cars, it had seemed to me easy, especially easy because I thought how it would stupefy her. Now I not only could not kill myself, but I could not even think of it.

'Why do it?' I asked myself, without answering.

Another knock at the door.

'Yes, but I must first know who is knocking. I have time enough.'

I put the revolver back on the table, and hid it under my newspaper. I went to the door and drew back the bolt.

It was my wife's sister, – a good and stupid widow.

'Basile, what does this mean?' said she, and her tears, always ready, began to flow.

'What do you want?' I asked roughly.

I saw clearly that there was no necessity of being rough with her, but I could not speak in any other tone.

'Basile, she is dying. Ivan Fedorowitch says so.'

Ivan Fedorowitch was the doctor, HER doctor, her counsellor.

'Is he here?' I inquired.

And all my hatred of her arose anew.

Well, what?

'Basile, go to her! Ah! how terrible it is!' said she.

'Go to her?' I asked myself; and immediately I made answer to myself that I ought to go, that probably that was the thing that is usually done when a husband like myself kills his wife, that it was absolutely necessary that I should go and see her.

'If that is the proper thing, I must go,' I repeated to myself. 'Yes, if it is necessary, I shall still have time,' said I to myself, thinking of my intention of blowing my brains out.

And I followed my sister-in-law. 'Now there are going to be phrases and grimaces, but I will not yield,' I declared to myself.

'Wait,' said I to my sister-in-law, 'it is stupid to be without boots. Let me at least put on my slippers.'"

# CHAPTER XXVIII

Strange thing! Again, when I had left my study, and was passing through the familiar rooms, again the hope came to me that nothing had happened. But the odor of the drugs, iodoform and phenic acid, brought me back to a sense of reality.

'No, everything has happened.'

In passing through the hall, beside the children's chamber, I saw little Lise. She was looking at me, with eyes that were full of fear. I even thought that all the children were looking at me. As I approached the door of our sleeping-room, a servant opened it from within, and came out. The first thing that I noticed was HER light gray dress upon a chair, all dark with blood. On our common bed she was stretched, with knees drawn up.

She lay very high, upon pillows, with her chemise half open. Linen had been placed upon the wound. A heavy smell of iodoform filled the room. Before, and more than anything else, I was astonished at her face, which was swollen and bruised under the eyes and over a part of the nose. This was the result of the blow that I had struck her with my elbow, when she had tried to hold me back. Of beauty there was no trace left. I saw something hideous in her. I stopped upon the threshold.

'Approach, approach her,' said her sister.

'Yes, probably she repents,' thought I; 'shall I forgive her? Yes, she is dying, I must forgive her,' I added, trying to be generous.

I approached the bedside. With difficulty she raised her eyes, one of which was swollen, and uttered these words haltingly:

'You have accomplished what you desired. You have killed me.'

And in her face, through the physical sufferings, in spite of the approach of death, was expressed the same old hatred, so familiar to me.

'The children . . . I will not give them to you . . . all the same . . . She (her sister) shall take them...'

But of that which I considered essential, of her fault, of her treason, one would have said that she did not think it necessary to say even a word.

'Yes, revel in what you have done.'

And she sobbed.

At the door stood her sister with the children.

'Yes, see what you have done!'

I cast a glance at the children, and then at her bruised and swollen face, and for the first time I forgot myself (my rights, my pride), and for the first time I saw in her a human being, a sister.

And all that which a moment before had been so offensive to me now seemed to me so petty, – all this jealousy, – and, on the contrary, what I had done seemed to me so important that I felt like bending over, approaching my face to her hand, and saying:

'Forgive me!'

But I did not dare. She was silent, with eyelids lowered, evidently having no strength to speak further. Then her deformed face began to tremble and shrivel, and she feebly pushed me back.

'Why has all this happened? Why?'

'Forgive me,' said I.

'Yes, if you had not killed me,' she cried suddenly, and her eyes shone feverishly. 'Forgiveness – that is nothing . . . If I only do not die! Ah, you have accomplished what you desired! I hate you!'

Then she grew delirious. She was frightened, and cried:

'Fire, I do not fear . . . but strike them all . . . He has gone . . . He has gone...'

"The delirium continued. She no longer recognized the children, not even little Lise, who had approached. Toward noon she died. As for me, I was arrested before her death, at eight o'clock in the morning. They took me to the police station, and then to prison, and there, during eleven months, awaiting the verdict, I reflected upon myself, and upon my past, and I understood it. Yes, I began to understand from the third day. The third day they took me to the house..."

Posdnicheff seemed to wish to add something, but, no longer having the strength to repress his sobs, he stopped. After a few minutes, having recovered his calmness, he resumed:

"I began to understand only when I saw her in the coffin..."

He uttered a sob, and then immediately continued, with haste:

"Then only, when I saw her dead face, did I understand all that I had done. I understood that it was I, I, who had killed her. I understood that I was the cause of the fact that she, who had been a moving, living, palpitating being, had now become motionless and cold, and that there was no way of repairing this thing. He who has not lived through that cannot understand it."

***

We remained silent a long time. Posdnicheff sobbed and trembled before me. His face had become delicate and long, and his mouth had grown larger.

"Yes," said he suddenly, "if I had known what I now know, I should never have married her, never, not for anything."

Again we remained silent for a long time.

"Yes, that is what I have done, that is my experience, We must understand the real meaning of the words of the Gospel, – Matthew, V. 28, – 'that whosoever looketh on a woman to lust after her hath committed adultery'; and these words relate to the wife, to the sister, and not only to the wife of another, but especially to one's own wife."

# CHAPTER XXIX

## LESSON OF THE KREUTZER SONATA.

***

I have received, and still continue to receive, numbers of letters from persons who are perfect strangers to me, asking me to state in plain and simple language my own views on the subject handled in the story entitled "The Kreutzer Sonata." With this request I shall now endeavor to comply.

My views on the question may be succinctly stated as follows: Without entering into details, it will be generally admitted that I am accurate in saying that many people condone in young men a course of conduct with regard to the other sex which is incompatible with strict morality, and that this dissoluteness is pardoned generally. Both parents and the government, in consequence of this view, may be said to wink at profligacy, and even in the last resource to encourage its practice. I am of opinion that this is not right.

It is not possible that the health of one class should necessitate the ruin of another, and, in consequence, it is our first duty to turn a deaf ear to such an essential immoral doctrine, no matter how strongly society may have established or law protected it. Moreover, it needs to be fully recognized that men are rightly to be held responsible for the consequences of their own acts, and that these are no longer to be visited on the woman alone. It follows from this that it is the duty of men who do not wish to lead a life of infamy to practice such continence in respect to all woman as they would were the female society in which they move made up exclusively of their own mothers and sisters.

A more rational mode of life should be adopted which would include abstinence from all alcoholic drinks, from excess in eating and from flesh meat, on the one hand, and recourse to physical labor on the other. I am not speaking of gymnastics, or of any of those occupations which may be fitly described as playing at work; I mean the genuine toil that fatigues. No one need go far in search of proofs that this kind of abstemious living is not merely possible, but far less hurtful to health than excess. Hundreds of instances are known to every one. This is my first contention.

In the second place, I think that of late years, through various reasons which I need not enter, but among which the above-mentioned laxity of opinion in society and the frequent idealization of the subject in current literature and painting may be mentioned, conjugal infidelity has become more common and is considered less reprehensible. I am of opinion that this is not right. The origin of the evil is twofold. It is due, in the first place, to a natural instinct, and, in the second, to the elevation of this instinct to a place to which it does not rightly belong. This being so, the evil can only be remedied by effecting a change in the views now in vogue about "falling in love" and all that this term implies, by educating men and women at home through family influence and example, and abroad by means of healthy public opinion, to practice that abstinence which morality and Christianity alike enjoin. This is my second contention.

In the third place I am of opinion that another consequence of the false light in which "falling in love," and what it leads to, are viewed in our society, is that the birth of children has lost its pristine significance, and that modern marriages are conceived less and less from the point of view of the family. I am of opinion that this is not right. This is my third contention.

In the fourth place, I am of opinion that the children (who in our society are considered an obstacle to enjoyment – an unlucky accident, as it were) are educated not with a view to the problem which they will be one day called on to face and to solve, but solely with an eye to the pleasure which they may be made to yield to their parents. The consequence is, that the children of human beings are brought up for all the world like the young of animals, the chief care of their parents being not to train them to such work as is worthy of men and women, but to increase their weight, or add a cubit to their stature, to make them spruce, sleek, well-fed, and comely. They rig them out in all manner of fantastic costumes, wash them, over-feed them, and refuse to make them work. If the children of the lower orders differ in this last respect from those of the well-to-do classes, the difference is merely formal; they work from sheer necessity, and not because their parents recognize work as a duty. And in over-fed children, as in over-fed animals, sensuality is engendered unnaturally early.

Fashionable dress to-day, the course of reading, plays, music, dances, luscious food, all the elements of our modern life, in a word, from the pictures on the little boxes of sweetmeats up to the novel, the tale, and the poem, contribute to fan this sensuality into a strong, consuming flame, with the result that sexual vices and diseases have come to be the normal conditions of the period of tender youth, and often continue into the riper age of full-blown manhood. And I am of opinion that this is not right.

It is high time it ceased. The children of human beings should not be brought up as if they were animals; and we should set up as the object and strive to maintain as the result of our labors something better and nobler than a well-dressed body. This is my fourth contention.

In the fifth place, I am of opinion that, owing to the exaggerated and erroneous significance attributed by our society to love and to the idealized states that accompany and succeed it, the best energies of our men and women are drawn forth and exhausted during the most promising period of life; those of the men in the work of looking for, choosing, and winning the most desirable objects of love, for which purpose lying and fraud are held to be quite excusable; those of the women and girls in alluring men and decoying them into liaisons or marriage by the most questionable means conceivable, as an instance of which the present fashions in evening dress may be cited. I am of opinion that this is not right.

The truth is, that the whole affair has been exalted by poets and romancers to an undue importance, and that love in its various developments is not a fitting object to consume the best energies of men. People set it before them and strive after it, because their view of life is as vulgar and brutish as is that other conception frequently met with in the lower stages of development, which sees in luscious and abundant food an end worthy of man's best efforts. Now, this is not right and should not be done. And, in order to avoid doing it, it is only needful to realize the fact that whatever truly deserves to be held up as a worthy object of man's striving and working, whether it be the service of humanity, of one's country, of science, of art, not to speak of the service of God, is far above and beyond the sphere of personal enjoyment. Hence, it follows that not only to form a liaison, but even to contract marriage, is, from a Christian point of view, not a progress, but a fall. Love, and all the states that accompany and follow it, however we may try in prose and verse to prove the contrary, never do and never can facilitate the attainment of an aim worthy of men, but always make it more difficult. This is my fifth contention.

How about the human race? If we admit that celibacy is better and nobler than marriage, evidently the human race will come to an end. But, if the logical conclusion of the argument is that the human race will become extinct, the whole reasoning is wrong.

To that I reply that the argument is not mine; I did not invent it. That it is incumbent on mankind so to strive, and that celibacy is preferable to marriage, are truths revealed by Christ 1,900 years ago, set forth in our catechisms, and professed by us as followers of Christ.

Chastity and celibacy, it is urged, cannot constitute the ideal of humanity, because chastity would annihilate the race which strove to realize it, and humanity cannot set up as its ideal its own annihilation. It may be pointed out in reply that only that is a true ideal, which, being unattainable, admits of infinite gradation in degrees of proximity. Such is the Christian ideal of the founding of God's kingdom, the union of all living creatures by the bonds of love. The conception of its attainment is incompatible with the conception of the movement of life. What kind of life could  subsist if all living creatures were joined  together by the bonds of love? None. Our conception of life is inseparably bound up with the conception of a continual striving after an unattainable  ideal.

But even if we suppose the Christian ideal of perfect chastity realized, what  then? We should merely find ourselves face to face on the one hand with the familiar teaching of religion, one of whose dogmas is that the world will have an end; and on the other of so-called science, which in- forms us that  the sun is gradually losing its heat, the result of which will in time be the extinction of the human race.

Now there is not and cannot be such an institution as Christian marriage, just as there cannot be such a thing as a Christian liturgy (Matt. vi. 5-12; John iv. 21), nor Christian teachers, nor church fathers (Matt. xxiii. 8-10), nor Christian armies, Christian law courts, nor Christian States. This is what was always taught and believed by true Christians of the first and following centuries. A Christian's ideal is not marriage, but love for God and for his neighbor. Consequently in the eyes of a Christian relations in marriage not only do not constitute a lawful, right, and happy state, as our society and our churches maintain, but, on the contrary, are always a fall.

Such a thing as Christian marriage never was and never could be. Christ did not marry, nor did he establish marriage; neither did his disciples marry. But if Christian marriage cannot exist, there is such a thing as a Christian view of marriage. And this is how it may be formulated: A Christian (and by this term I understand not those who call themselves Christians merely because they were baptized and still receive the sacrament once a year, but those whose lives are shaped and regulated by the teachings of Christ), I say, cannot view the marriage relation otherwise than as a deviation from the doctrine of Christ, – as a sin. This is clearly laid down in Matt. v. 28, and the ceremony called Christian marriage does not alter its character one jot. A Christian will never, therefore, desire marriage, but will always avoid it.

If the light of truth dawns upon a Christian when he is already married, or if, being a Christian, from weakness he enters into marital relations with the ceremonies of the church, or without them, he has no other alternative than to abide with his wife (and the wife with her husband, if it is she who is a Christian) and to aspire together with her to free themselves of their sin. This is the Christian view of marriage; and there cannot be any other for a man who honestly endeavors to shape his life in accordance with the teachings of Christ.

To very many persons the thoughts I have uttered here and in "The Kreutzer Sonata" will seem strange, vague, even contradictory. They certainly do contradict, not each other, but the whole tenor of our lives, and involuntarily a doubt arises, "on which side is truth, – on the side of the thoughts which seem true and well-founded, or on the side of the lives of others and myself?" I, too, was weighed down by that same doubt when writing "The Kreutzer Sonata." I had not the faintest presentiment that the train of thought I had started would lead me whither it did. I was terrified by my own conclusion, and I was at first disposed to reject it, but it was impossible not to hearken to the voice of my reason and my conscience. And so, strange though they may appear to many, opposed as they undoubtedly are to the trend and tenor of our lives, and incompatible though they may prove with what I have heretofore thought and uttered, I have no choice but to accept them. "But man is weak," people will object. "His task should be regulated by his strength."

This is tantamount to saying, "My hand is weak. I cannot draw a straight line, – that is, a line which will be the shortest line between two given points, – and so, in order to make it more easy for myself, I, intending to draw a straight, will choose for my model a crooked line."

The weaker my hand, the greater the need that my model should be perfect.

LEO TOLSTOI.

# STORY 2

## IVAN THE FOOL

***

# CHAPTER I

In a certain kingdom there lived a rich peasant, who had three sons – Simeon (a soldier), Tarras-Briukhan (fat man), and Ivan (a fool) – and one daughter, Milania, born dumb. Simeon went to war, to serve the Czar; Tarras went to a city and became a merchant; and Ivan, with his sister, remained at home to work on the farm.

For his valiant service in the army, Simeon received an estate with high rank, and married a noble's daughter. Besides his large pay, he was in receipt of a handsome income from his estate; yet he was unable to make ends meet. What the husband saved, the wife wasted in extravagance. One day Simeon went to the estate to collect his income, when the steward informed him that there was no income, saying:

"We have neither horses, cows, fishing-nets, nor implements; it is necessary first to buy everything, and then to look for income."

Simeon thereupon went to his father and said:

"You are rich, batiushka,[4] but you have given nothing to me. Give me one-third of what you possess as my share, and I will transfer it to my estate."

The old man replied: "You did not help to bring prosperity to our household. For what reason, then, should you now demand the third part of everything? It would be unjust to Ivan and his sister."

"Yes," said Simeon; "but he is a fool, and she was born dumb. What need have they of anything?"

"See what Ivan will say."

Ivan's reply was: "Well, let him take his share."

Simeon took the portion allotted to him, and went again to serve in the army.

---

4  little father

Tarras also met with success. He became rich and married a merchant's daughter, but even this failed to satisfy his desires, and he also went to his father and said, "Give me my share."

The old man, however, refused to comply with his request, saying: "You had no hand in the accumulation of our property, and what our household contains is the result of Ivan's hard work. It would be unjust," he repeated, "to Ivan and his sister."

Tarras replied: "But he does not need it. He is a fool, and cannot marry, for no one will have him; and sister does not require anything, for she was born dumb." Turning then to Ivan he continued: "Give me half the grain you have, and I will not touch the implements or fishing-nets; and from the cattle I will take only the dark mare, as she is not fit to plow."

Ivan laughed and said: "Well, I will go and arrange matters so that Tarras may have his share," whereupon Tarras took the brown mare with the grain to town, leaving Ivan with one old horse to work on as before and support his father, mother, and sister.

# CHAPTER II

It was disappointing to the Stary Tchert (Old Devil) that the brothers did not quarrel over the division of the property, and that they separated peacefully; and he cried out, calling his three small devils (Tchertionki).

"See here," said he, "there are living three brothers – Simeon the soldier, Tarras-Briukhan, and Ivan the Fool. It is necessary that they should quarrel. Now they live peacefully, and enjoy each other's hospitality. The Fool spoiled all my plans. Now you three go and work with them in such a manner that they will be ready to tear each other's eyes out. Can you do this?"

"We can," they replied.

"How will you accomplish it?"

"In this way: We will first ruin them to such an extent that they will have nothing to eat, and we will then gather them together in one place where we are sure that they will fight."

"Very well; I see you understand your business. Go, and do not return to me until you have created a feud between the three brothers – or I will skin you alive."

The three small devils went to a swamp to consult as to the best means of accomplishing their mission. They disputed for a long time – each one wanting the easiest part of the work – and not being able to agree, concluded to draw lots; by which it was decided that the one who was first finished had to come and help the others. This agreement being entered into, they appointed a time when they were again to meet in the swamp – to find out who was through and who needed assistance.

The time having arrived, the young devils met in the swamp as agreed, when each related his experience. The first, who went to Simeon, said: "I have succeeded in my undertaking, and to-morrow Simeon returns to his father."

His comrades, eager for particulars, inquired how he had done it.

"Well," he began, "the first thing I did was to blow some courage into his veins, and, on the strength of it, Simeon went to the Czar and offered to conquer the whole world for him. The Emperor made him commander-in-chief of the forces, and sent him with an army to fight the Viceroy of India. Having started on their mission of conquest, they were unaware that I, following in their wake, had wet all their powder. I also went to the Indian ruler and showed him how I could create numberless soldiers from straw."

"Simeon's army, seeing that they were surrounded by such a vast number of Indian warriors of my creation, became frightened, and Simeon commanded to fire from cannons and rifles, which of course they were unable to do. The soldiers, discouraged, retreated in great disorder. Thus Simeon brought upon himself the terrible disgrace of defeat.

His estate was confiscated, and to-morrow he is to be executed. All that remains for me to do, therefore," concluded the young devil, "is to release him to-morrow morning. Now, then, who wants my assistance?"

The second small devil (from Tarras) then related his story.

"I do not need any help," he began. "My business is also all right. My work with Tarras will be finished in one week. In the first place I made him grow thin. He afterward became so covetous that he wanted to possess everything he saw, and he spent all the money he had in the purchase of immense quantities of goods. When his capital was gone he still continued to buy with borrowed money, and has become involved in such difficulties that he cannot free himself. At the end of one week the date for the payment of his notes will have expired, and, his goods being seized upon, he will become a bankrupt; and he also will return to his father."

At the conclusion of this narrative they inquired of the third devil how things had fared between him and Ivan.

"Well," said he, "my report is not so encouraging. The first thing I did was to spit into his jug of quass,[5] which made him sick at his stomach. He afterward went to plow his summer-fallow, but I made the soil so hard that the plow could scarcely penetrate it. I thought the Fool would not succeed, but he started to work nevertheless. Moaning with pain, he still continued to labor. I broke one plow, but he replaced it with another, fixing it securely, and resumed work. Going beneath the surface of the ground I took hold of the plowshares, but did not succeed in stopping Ivan. He pressed so hard, and the colter was so sharp, that my hands were cut; and despite my utmost efforts, he went over all but a small portion of the field."

He concluded with: "Come, brothers, and help me, for if we do not conquer him our

---

[5] a sour drink made from rye

whole enterprise will be a failure. If the Fool is permitted successfully to conduct his farming, they will have no need, for he will support his brothers."

# CHAPTER III

Ivan having succeeded in plowing all but a small portion of his land, he returned the next day to finish it. The pain in his stomach continued, but he felt that he must go on with his work. He tried to start his plow, but it would not move; it seemed to have struck a hard root. It was the small devil in the ground who had wound his feet around the plowshares and held them.

"This is strange," thought Ivan. "There were never any roots here before, and this is surely one."

Ivan put his hand in the ground, and, feeling something soft, grasped and pulled it out. It was like a root in appearance, but seemed to possess life. Holding it up he saw that it was a little devil. Disgusted, he exclaimed, "See the nasty thing," and he proceeded to strike it a blow, intending to kill it, when the young devil cried out:

"Do not kill me, and I will grant your every wish."

"What can you do for me?"

"Tell me what it is you most wish for," the little devil replied.

Ivan, peasant-fashion, scratched the back of his head as he thought, and finally he said:

"I am dreadfully sick at my stomach. Can you cure me?"

"I can," the little devil said.

"Then do so."

The little devil bent toward the earth and began searching for roots, and when he found them he gave them to Ivan, saying: "If you will swallow some of these you will be immediately cured of whatsoever disease you are afflicted with."

Ivan did as directed, and obtained instant relief.

"I beg of you to let me go now," the little devil pleaded; "I will pass into the earth, never to return."

"Very well; you may go, and God bless you;" and as Ivan pronounced the name of God, the small devil disappeared into the earth like a flash, and only a slight opening in the ground remained.

Ivan placed in his hat what roots he had left, and proceeded to plow. Soon finishing his work, he turned his plow over and returned home.

When he reached the house he found his brother Simeon and his wife seated at the supper-table. His estate had been confiscated, and he himself had barely escaped execution by making his way out of prison, and having nothing to live upon had come back to his father for support.

Turning to Ivan he said: "I came to ask you to care for us until I can find something to do."

"Very well," Ivan replied; "you may remain with us."

Just as Ivan was about to sit down to the table Simeon's wife made a wry face, indicating that she did not like the smell of Ivan's sheep-skin coat; and turning to her husband she said, "I shall not sit at the table with a moujik[6] who smells like that."

Simeon the soldier turned to his brother and said: "My lady objects to the smell of your clothes. You may eat in the porch."

Ivan said: "Very well, it is all the same to me. I will soon have to go and feed my horse any way."

---

6   peasant

Ivan took some bread in one hand, and his kaftan (coat) in the other, and left the room.

# CHAPTER IV

The small devil finished with Simeon that night, and according to agreement went to the assistance of his comrade who had charge of Ivan, that he might help to conquer the Fool. He went to the field and searched everywhere, but could find nothing but the hole through which the small devil had disappeared.

"Well, this is strange," he said; "something must have happened to my companion, and I will have to take his place and continue the work he began. The Fool is through with his plowing, so I must look about me for some other means of compassing his destruction. I must overflow his meadow and prevent him from cutting the grass."

The little devil accordingly overflowed the meadow with muddy water, and, when Ivan went at dawn next morning with his scythe set and sharpened and tried to mow the grass, he found that it resisted all his efforts and would not yield to the implement as usual.

Many times Ivan tried to cut the grass, but always without success. At last, becoming weary of the effort, he decided to return home and have his scythe again sharpened, and also to procure a quantity of bread, saying: "I will come back here and will not leave until I have mown all the meadow, even if it should take a whole week."

Hearing this, the little devil became thoughtful, saying: "That Ivan is a koolak,[7] and I must think of some other way of conquering him."

Ivan soon returned with his sharpened scythe and started to mow.

The small devil hid himself in the grass, and as the point of the scythe came down he buried it in the earth and made it almost impossible for Ivan

---

7  hard case

to move the implement. He, however, succeeded in mowing all but one small spot in the swamp, where again the small devil hid himself, saying: "Even if he should cut my hands I will prevent him from accomplishing his work."

When Ivan came to the swamp he found that the grass was not very thick. Still, the scythe would not work, which made him so angry that he worked with all his might, and one blow more powerful than the others cut off a portion of the small devil's tail, who had hidden himself there.

Despite the little devil's efforts he succeeded in finishing his work, when he returned home and ordered his sister to gather up the grass while he went to another field to cut rye. But the devil preceded him there, and fixed the rye in such a manner that it was almost impossible for Ivan to cut it; however, after continuous hard labor he succeeded, and when he was through with the rye he said to himself: "Now I will start to mow oats."

On hearing this, the little devil thought to himself: "I could not prevent him from mowing the rye, but I will surely stop him from mowing the oats when the morning comes."

Early next day, when the devil came to the field, he found that the oats had been already mowed. Ivan did it during the night, so as to avoid the loss that might have resulted from the grain being too ripe and dry. Seeing that Ivan again had escaped him, the little devil became greatly enraged, saying:

"He cut me all over and made me tired, that fool. I did not meet such misfortune even on the battle-field. He does not even sleep;" and the devil began to swear. "I cannot follow him," he continued. "I will go now to the heaps and make everything rotten."

Accordingly he went to a heap of the new-mown grain and began his fiendish work. After wetting it he built a fire and warmed himself, and soon was fast asleep.

Ivan harnessed his horse, and, with his sister, went to bring the rye home from the field.

After lifting a couple of sheaves from the first heap his pitchfork came into contact with the little devil's back, which caused the latter to howl with pain and to jump around in every direction. Ivan exclaimed:

"See here! What nastiness! You again here?"

"I am another one!" said the little devil. "That was my brother. I am the one who was sent to your brother Simeon."

"Well," said Ivan, "it matters not who you are. I will fix you all the same."

As Ivan was about to strike the first blow the devil pleaded: "Let me go and I will do you no more harm. I will do whatever you wish."

"What can you do for me?" asked Ivan.

"I can make soldiers from almost anything."

"And what will they be good for?"

"Oh, they will do everything for you!"

"Can they sing?"

"They can."

"Well, make them."

"Take a bunch of straw and scatter it on the ground, and see if each straw will not turn into a soldier."

Ivan shook the straws on the ground, and, as he expected, each straw turned into a soldier, and they began marching with a band at their head.

"Ishty,[8] that was well done! How it will delight the village maidens!" he exclaimed.

The small devil now said: "Let me go; you do not need me any longer."

But Ivan said: "No, I will not let you go just yet. You have converted the straw into soldiers, and now I want you to turn them again into straw, as I cannot afford to lose it, but I want it with the grain on."

The devil replied: "Say: 'So many soldiers, so much straw.'"

Ivan did as directed, and got back his rye with the straw.

The small devil again begged for his release.

Ivan, taking him from the pitchfork, said: "With God's blessing you may depart"; and, as before at the mention

---

8  look you

of God's name, the little devil was hurled into the earth like a flash, and nothing was left but the hole to show where he had gone.

Soon afterward Ivan returned home, to find his brother Tarras and his wife there. Tarras-Briukhan could not pay his debts, and was forced to flee from his creditors and seek refuge under his father's roof. Seeing Ivan, he said: "Well, Ivan, may we remain here until I start in some new business?"

Ivan replied as he had before to Simeon: "Yes, you are perfectly welcome to remain here as long as it suits you."

With that announcement he removed his coat and seated himself at the supper-table with the others. But Tarras-Briukhan's wife objected to the smell of his clothes, saying: "I cannot eat with a fool; neither can I stand the smell."

Then Tarras-Briukhan said: "Ivan, from your clothes there comes a bad smell; go and eat by yourself in the porch."

"Very well," said Ivan; and he took some bread and went out as ordered, saying, "It is time for me to feed my mare."

# CHAPTER V

The small devil who had charge of Tarras finished with him that night, and according to agreement proceeded to the assistance of the other two to help them conquer Ivan. Arriving at the plowed field he looked around for his comrades, but found only the hole through which one had disappeared; and on going to the meadow he discovered the severed tail of the other, and in the rye-field he found yet another hole.

"Well," he thought, "it is quite clear that my comrades have met with some great misfortune, and that I will have to take their places and arrange the feud between the brothers."

The small devil then went in search of Ivan. But he, having finished with the field, was nowhere to be found. He had gone to the forest to cut logs to build homes for his brothers, as they found it inconvenient for so many to live under the same roof.

The small devil at last discovered his whereabouts, and going to the forest climbed into the branches of the trees and began to interfere with Ivan's work. Ivan cut down a tree, which failed, however, to fall to the ground, becoming entangled in the branches of other trees; yet he succeeded in getting it down after a hard struggle. In chopping down the next tree he met with the same difficulties, and also with the third. Ivan had supposed he could cut down fifty trees in a day, but he succeeded in chopping but ten before darkness put an end to his labors for a time. He was now exhausted, and, perspiring profusely, he sat down alone in the woods to rest. He soon after resumed his work, cutting down one more tree; but the effort gave him a pain in his back, and he was obliged to rest again. Seeing this, the small devil was full of joy.

"Well," he thought, "now he is exhausted and will stop work, and I will rest also." He then seated himself on some branches and rejoiced.

Ivan again arose, however, and, taking his axe, gave the tree a terrific blow from the opposite side, which felled it instantly to the ground, carrying the little devil with it; and Ivan, proceeding to cut the branches, found the devil alive. Very much astonished, Ivan exclaimed:

"Look you! Such nastiness! Are you again here?"

"I am another one," replied the devil. "I was with your brother Tarras."

"Well," said Ivan, "that makes no difference; I will fix you." And he was about to strike him a blow with the axe when the devil pleaded:

"Do not kill me, and whatever you wish you shall have."

Ivan asked, "What can you do?"

"I can make for you all the money you wish."

Ivan then told the devil he might proceed, whereupon the latter began to explain to him how he might become rich.

"Take," said he to Ivan, "the leaves of this oak tree and rub them in your hands, and the gold will fall to the ground."

Ivan did as he was directed, and immediately the gold began to drop about his feet; and he remarked:

"This will be a fine trick to amuse the village boys with."

"Can I now take my departure?" asked the devil, to which Ivan replied, "With God's blessing you may go."

At the mention of the name of God, the devil disappeared into the earth.

# CHAPTER VI

The brothers, having finished their houses, moved into them and lived apart from their father and brother. Ivan, when he had completed his plowing, made a great feast, to which he invited his brothers, telling them that he had plenty of beer for them to drink. The brothers, however, declined Ivan's hospitality, saying, "We have seen the beer moujiks drink, and want none of it."

Ivan then gathered around him all the peasants in the village and with them drank beer until he became intoxicated, when he joined the Khorovody (a street gathering of the village boys and girls, who sing songs), and told them they must sing his praises, saying that in return he would show them such sights as they had never before seen in their lives. The little girls laughed and began to sing songs praising Ivan, and when they had finished they said: "Very well; now give us what you said you would."

Ivan replied, "I will soon show you," and, taking an empty bag in his hand, he started for the woods. The little girls laughed as they said, "What a fool he is!" and resuming their play they forgot all about him.

Some time after Ivan suddenly appeared among them carrying in his hand the bag, which was now filled.

"Shall I divide this with you?" he said.

"Yes; divide!" they sang in chorus.

So Ivan put his hand into the bag and drew it out full of gold coins, which he scattered among them.

"Batiushka," they cried as they ran to gather up the precious pieces.

The moujiks then appeared on the scene and began to fight among themselves for the possession of the yellow objects. In the melee one old woman was nearly crushed to death.

Ivan laughed and was greatly amused at the sight of so many persons quarrelling over a few pieces of gold.

"Oh! you duratchki" (little fools), he said, "why did you almost crush the life out of the old grandmother? Be more gentle. I have plenty more, and I will give them to you;" whereupon he began throwing about more of the coins.

The people gathered around him, and Ivan continued throwing until he emptied his bag. They clamored for more, but Ivan replied: "The gold is all gone. Another time I will give you more. Now we will resume our singing and dancing."

The little children sang, but Ivan said to them, "Your songs are no good."

The children said, "Then show us how to sing better."

To this Ivan replied, "I will show you people who can sing better than you." With that remark Ivan went to the barn and, securing a bundle of straw, did as the little devil had directed him; and presently a regiment of soldiers appeared in the village street, and he ordered them to sing and dance.

The people were astonished and could not understand how Ivan had produced the strangers.

The soldiers sang for some time, to the great delight of the villagers; and when Ivan commanded them to stop they instantly ceased.

Ivan then ordered them off to the barn, telling the astonished and mystified moujiks that they must not follow him. Reaching the barn, he turned the soldiers again into straw and went home to sleep off the effects of his debauch.

# CHAPTER VII

The next morning Ivan's exploits were the talk of the village, and news of the wonderful things he had done reached the ears of his brother Simeon, who immediately went to Ivan to learn all about it.

"Explain to me," he said; "from whence did you bring the soldiers, and where did you take them?"

"And what do you wish to know for?" asked Ivan.

"Why, with soldiers we can do almost anything we wish – whole kingdoms can be conquered," replied Simeon.

This information greatly surprised Ivan, who said: "Well, why did you not tell me about this before? I can make as many as you want."

Ivan then took his brother to the barn, but he said: "While I am willing to create the soldiers, you must take them away from here; for if it should become necessary to feed them, all the food in the village would last them only one day."

Simeon promised to do as Ivan wished, whereupon Ivan proceeded to convert the straw into soldiers. Out of one bundle of straw he made an entire regiment; in fact, so many soldiers appeared as if by magic that there was not a vacant spot in the field.

Turning to Simeon Ivan said, "Well, is there a sufficient number?"

Beaming with joy, Simeon replied: "Enough! enough! Thank you, Ivan!"

"Glad you are satisfied," said Ivan, "and if you wish more I will make them for you. I have plenty of straw now."

Simeon divided his soldiers into battalions and regiments, and after having drilled them he went forth to fight and to conquer.

Simeon had just gotten safely out of the village with his soldiers when Tarras, the other brother, appeared before Ivan – he also having heard of the previous day's performance and wanting to learn the secret of his power. He sought Ivan, saying: "Tell me the secret of your supply of gold, for if I had plenty of money I could with its assistance gather in all the wealth in the world."

Ivan was greatly surprised on hearing this statement, and said: "You might have told me this before, for I can obtain for you as much money as you wish."

Tarras was delighted, and he said, "You might get me about three bushels."

"Well," said Ivan, "we will go to the woods, or, better still, we will harness the horse, as we could not possibly carry so much money ourselves."

The brothers went to the woods and Ivan proceeded to gather the oak leaves, which he rubbed between his hands, the dust falling to the ground and turning into gold pieces as quickly as it fell.

When quite a pile had accumulated Ivan turned to Tarras and asked if he had rubbed enough leaves into money, whereupon Tarras replied: "Thank you, Ivan; that will be sufficient for this time."

Ivan then said: "If you wish more, come to me and I will rub as much as you want, for there are plenty of leaves."

Tarras, with his tarantas (wagon) filled with gold, rode away to the city to engage in trade and increase his wealth; and thus both brothers went their way, Simeon to fight and Tarras to trade.

Simeon's soldiers conquered a kingdom for him and Tarras-Briukhan made plenty of money.

Some time afterward the two brothers met and confessed to each other the source from whence sprang their prosperity, but they were not yet satisfied.

Simeon said: "I have conquered a kingdom and enjoy a very pleasant life, but I have not sufficient money to procure food for my soldiers;" while Tarras confessed that he was the possessor of enormous wealth, but the care of it caused him much uneasiness.

"Let us go again to our brother," said Simeon; "I will order him to make more soldiers and will give them to you, and you may then tell him that he must make more money so that we can buy food for them."

They went again to Ivan, and Simeon said: "I have not sufficient soldiers; I want you to make me at least two divisions more." But Ivan shook his head as he said: "I will not create soldiers for nothing; you must pay me for doing it."

"Well, but you promised," said Simeon.

"I know I did," replied Ivan; "but I have changed my mind since that time."

"But, fool, why will you not do as you promised?"

"For the reason that your soldiers kill men, and I will not make any more for such a cruel purpose." With this reply Ivan remained stubborn and would not create any more soldiers.

Tarras-Briukhan next approached Ivan and ordered him to make more money; but, as in the case of Tarras, Ivan only shook his head, as he said: "I will not make you any money unless you pay me for doing it. I cannot work without pay."

Tarras then reminded him of his promise.

"I know I promised," replied Ivan; "but still I must refuse to do as you wish."

"But why, fool, will you not fulfill your promise?" asked Tarras.

"For the reason that your gold was the means of depriving Mikhailovna of her cow."

"But how did that happen?" inquired Tarras.

"It happened in this way," said Ivan. "Mikhailovna always kept a cow, and her children had plenty of milk to drink; but some time ago one of her boys came to me to beg for some milk, and I asked, 'Where is your cow?' when he replied, 'A clerk of Tarras-Briukhan came to our home and offered three gold pieces for her. Our mother could not resist the temptation, and now we have no milk to drink. I gave you the gold pieces for your pleasure, and you put them to such poor use that I will not give you any more.'"

The brothers, on hearing this, took their departure to discuss as to the best plan to pursue in regard to a settlement of their troubles.

Simeon said: "Let us arrange it in this way: I will give you the half of my kingdom, and soldiers to keep guard over your wealth; and you give me money to feed the soldiers in my half of the kingdom."

To this arrangement Tarras agreed, and both the brothers became rulers and very happy.

# CHAPTER VIII

Ivan remained on the farm and worked to support his father, mother, and dumb sister. Once it happened that the old dog, which had grown up on the farm, was taken sick, when Ivan thought he was dying, and, taking pity on the animal, placed some bread in his hat and carried it to him. It happened that when he turned out the bread the root which the little devil had given him fell out also. The old dog swallowed it with the bread and was almost instantly cured, when he jumped up and began to wag his tail as an expression of joy. Ivan's father and mother, seeing the dog cured so quickly, asked by what means he had performed such a miracle.

Ivan replied: "I had some roots which would cure any disease, and the dog swallowed one of them."

It happened about that time that the Czar's daughter became ill, and her father had it announced in every city, town, and village that whosoever would cure her would be richly rewarded; and if the lucky person should prove to be a single man he would give her in marriage to him.

This announcement, of course, appeared in Ivan's village.

Ivan's father and mother called him and said: "If you have any of those wonderful roots, go and cure the Czar's daughter. You will be much happier for having performed such a kind act – indeed, you will be made happy for all your after life."

"Very well," said Ivan; and he immediately made ready for the journey. As he reached the porch on his way out he saw a poor woman standing directly in his path and holding a broken arm. The woman accosted him, saying:

"I was told that you could cure me, and will you not please do so, as I am powerless to do anything for myself?"

Ivan replied: "Very well, my poor woman; I will relieve you if I can."

He produced a root which he handed to the poor woman and told her to swallow it.

She did as Ivan told her and was instantly cured, and went away rejoicing that she had recovered the use of her arm.

Ivan's father and mother came out to wish him good luck on his journey, and to them he told the story of the poor woman, saying that he had given her his last root. On hearing this his parents were much distressed, as they now believed him to be without the means of curing the Czar's daughter, and began to scold him.

"You had pity for a beggar and gave no thought to the Czar's daughter," they said.

"I have pity for the Czar's daughter also," replied Ivan, after which he harnessed his horse to his wagon and took his seat ready for his departure; whereupon his parents said: "Where are you going, you fool – to cure the Czar's daughter, and without anything to do it with?"

"Very well," replied Ivan, as he drove away.

In due time he arrived at the palace, and the moment he appeared on the balcony the Czar's daughter was cured. The Czar was overjoyed and ordered Ivan to be brought into his presence. He dressed him in the richest robes and addressed him as his son-in-law. Ivan was married to the Czarevna, and, the Czar dying soon after, Ivan became ruler. Thus the three brothers became rulers in different kingdoms.

# CHAPTER IX

The brothers lived and reigned. Simeon, the eldest brother, with his straw soldiers took captive the genuine soldiers and trained all alike. He was feared by every one.

Tarras-Briukhan, the other brother, did not squander the gold he obtained from Ivan, but instead greatly increased his wealth, and at the same time lived well. He kept his money in large trunks, and, while having more than he knew what to do with, still continued to collect money from his subjects. The people had to work for the money to pay the taxes which Tarras levied on them, and life was made burdensome to them.

Ivan the Fool did not enjoy his wealth and power to the same extent as did his brothers. As soon as his father-in-law, the late Czar, was buried, he discarded the Imperial robes which had fallen to him and told his wife to put them away, as he had no further use for them. Having cast aside the insignia of his rank, he once more donned his peasant garb and started to work as of old.

"I felt lonesome," he said, "and began to grow enormously stout, and yet I had no appetite, and neither could I sleep."

Ivan sent for his father, mother, and dumb sister, and brought them to live with him, and they worked with him at whatever he chose to do.

The people soon learned that Ivan was a fool. His wife one day said to him, "The people say you are a fool, Ivan."

"Well, let them think so if they wish," he replied.

His wife pondered this reply for some time, and at last decided that if Ivan was a fool she also was one, and that it would be useless to go contrary to her husband, thinking affectionately of the old proverb that "where the needle goes there goes the thread also." She therefore cast aside her magnificent robes, and, putting them into the trunk with Ivan's, dressed herself in cheap clothing and joined her dumb sister-in-law, with the intention of learning to work. She succeeded so well that she soon became a great help to Ivan.

Seeing that Ivan was a fool, all the wise men left the kingdom and only the fools remained. They had no money, their wealth consisting only of the products of their labor. But they lived peacefully together, supported themselves in comfort, and had plenty to spare for the needy and afflicted.

# CHAPTER X

The old devil grew tired of waiting for the good news which he expected the little devils to bring him. He waited in vain to hear of the ruin of the brothers, so he went in search of the emissaries which he had sent to perform that work for him. After looking around for some time, and seeing nothing but the three holes in the ground, he decided that they had not succeeded in their work and that he would have to do it himself.

The old devil next went in search of the brothers, but he could learn nothing of their whereabouts. After some time he found them in their different kingdoms, contented and happy. This greatly incensed the old devil, and he said, "I will now have to accomplish their mission myself."

He first visited Simeon the soldier, and appeared before him as a voyevoda (general), saying: "You, Simeon, are a great warrior, and I also have had considerable experience in warfare, and am desirous of serving you."

Simeon questioned the disguised devil, and seeing that he was an intelligent man took him into his service.

The new General taught Simeon how to strengthen his army until it became very powerful. New implements of warfare were introduced.

Cannons capable of throwing one hundred balls a minute were also constructed, and these, it was expected, would be of deadly effect in battle.

Simeon, on the advice of his new General, ordered all young men above a certain age to report for drill. On the same advice Simeon established gun-shops, where immense numbers of cannons and rifles were made.

The next move of the new General was to have Simeon declare war against the neighboring kingdom. This he did, and with his immense army marched into the adjoining territory, which he pillaged and burned, destroying more than half the enemy's soldiers. This so frightened the ruler of that country that he willingly gave up half of his kingdom to save the other half.

Simeon, overjoyed at his success, declared his intention of marching into Indian territory and subduing the Viceroy of that country.

But Simeon's intentions reached the ears of the Indian ruler, who prepared to do battle with him. In addition to having secured all the latest implements of warfare, he added still others of his own invention. He ordered all boys over fourteen and all single women to be drafted into the army, until its proportions became much larger than Simeon's. His cannons and rifles were of the same pattern as Simeon's, and he invented a flying-machine from which bombs could be thrown into the enemy's camp.

Simeon went forth to conquer the Viceroy with full confidence in his own powers to succeed. This time luck forsook him, and instead of being the conqueror he was himself conquered.

The Indian ruler had so arranged his army that Simeon could not even get within shooting distance, while the bombs from the flying-machine carried destruction and terror in their path, completely routing his army, so that Simeon was left alone.

The Viceroy took possession of his kingdom and Simeon had to fly for his life.

Having finished with Simeon, the old devil   next approached Tarras. He appeared before him disguised as one of the merchants of his kingdom, and established factories and began to make money. The "merchant" paid the highest price for everything he purchased, and the people ran after him to sell their goods. Through this "merchant" they were enabled to make plenty of money, paying up all their arrears of taxes as well as the others when they came due.

Tarras was overjoyed at this condition of affairs and said: "Thanks to this merchant, now I will have more money than before, and life will be much pleasanter for me."

He wished to erect new buildings, and advertised for workmen, offering the highest prices for all kinds of labor. Tarras thought the people would be as anxious to work as formerly, but instead he was much surprised to learn that they were working for the "merchant." Thinking to induce them to leave the "merchant," he increased his offers, but the former, equal to the emergency, also raised the wages of his workmen. Tarras, having plenty of money, increased the offers still more; but the "merchant" raised them still higher and got the better of him. Thus, defeated at every point, Tarras was compelled to abandon the idea of building.

Tarras next announced that he intended laying out gardens and erecting fountains, and the work was to be commenced in the fall, but no one came to offer his services, and again he was obliged to forego his intentions. Winter set in, and Tarras wanted some sable fur with which to line his great-coat, and he sent his man to procure it for him; but the servant returned without it, saying: "There are no sables to be had. The 'merchant' has bought them all, paying a very high price for them."

Tarras needed horses and sent a messenger to purchase them, but he returned with the same story as on former occasions – that none were to be found, the "merchant" having bought them all to carry water for an artificial pond he was constructing. Tarras was at last compelled to suspend business, as he could not find any one willing to work for him. They had all gone over to the "merchant's" side. The only dealings the people had with Tarras were when they went to pay their taxes. His money accumulated so fast that he could not find a place to put it, and his life became miserable. He abandoned all idea of entering upon the new venture, and only thought of how to exist peaceably. This he found it difficult to do, for, turn which way he would, fresh obstacles confronted him. Even his cooks, coachmen, and all his other servants forsook him and joined the "merchant." With all his wealth he had nothing to eat, and when he went to market he found the "merchant" had been there before him and had bought up all the provisions. Still, the people continued to bring him money.

Tarras at last became so indignant that he ordered the "merchant" out of his kingdom. He left, but settled just outside the boundary line, and continued his business with the same result as before, and Tarras was frequently forced to go without food for days. It was rumored that the "merchant" wanted to buy even Tarras himself. On hearing this the latter became very much alarmed and could not decide as to the best course to pursue.

About this time his brother Simeon arrived in the kingdom, and said: "Help me, for I have been defeated and ruined by the Indian Viceroy."

Tarras replied: "How can I help you, when I have had no food myself for two days?"

# CHAPTER XI

The old devil, having finished with the second brother, went to Ivan the Fool. This time he disguised himself as a General, the same as in the case of Simeon, and, appearing before Ivan, said: "Get an army together. It is disgraceful for the ruler of a kingdom to be without an army. You call your people to assemble, and I will form them into a fine large army."

Ivan took the supposed General's advice, and said: "Well, you may form my people into an army, but you must also teach them to sing the songs I like."

The old devil then went through Ivan's kingdom to secure recruits for the army, saying: "Come, shave your heads and I will give each of you a red hat and plenty of vodki" (whiskey).

At this the fools only laughed, and said: "We can have all the vodki we want, for we distill it ourselves; and of hats, our little girls make all we want, of any color we please, and with handsome fringes."

Thus was the devil foiled in securing recruits for his army; so he returned to Ivan and said: "Your fools will not volunteer to be soldiers. It will therefore be necessary to force them."

"Very well," replied Ivan, "you may use force if you want to."

The old devil then announced that all the fools must become soldiers, and those who refused, Ivan would punish with death.

The fools went to the General; and said: "You tell us that Ivan will punish with death all those who refuse to become soldiers, but you have omitted to state what will be done with us soldiers. We have been told that we are only to be killed."

"Yes, that is true," was the reply.

The fools on hearing this became stubborn and refused to go.

"Better kill us now if we cannot avoid death, but we will not become soldiers," they declared.

"Oh! you fools," said the old devil, "soldiers may and may not be killed; but if you disobey Ivan's orders you will find certain death at his hands."

The fools remained absorbed in thought for some time and finally went to Ivan to question him in regard to the matter.

On arriving at his house they said: "A General came to us with an order from you that we were all to become soldiers, and if we refused you were to punish us with death. Is it true?"

Ivan began to laugh heartily on hearing this, and said: "Well, how I alone can punish you with death is something I cannot understand. If I was not a fool myself I would be able to explain it to you, but as it is I cannot."

"Well, then, we will not go," they said.

"Very well," replied Ivan, "you need not become soldiers unless you wish to."

The old devil, seeing his schemes about to prove failures, went to the ruler of Tarakania and became his friend, saying: "Let us go and conquer Ivan's kingdom. He has no money, but he has plenty of cattle, provisions, and various other things that would be useful to us."

The Tarakanian ruler gathered his large army together, and equipping it with cannons and rifles, crossed the boundary line into Ivan's kingdom. The people went to Ivan and said: "The ruler of Tarakania is here with a large army to fight us."

"Let them come," replied Ivan.

The Tarakanian ruler, after crossing the line into Ivan's kingdom, looked in vain for soldiers to fight against; and waiting some time and none appearing, he sent his own warriors to attack the villages.

They soon reached the first village, which they began to plunder.

The fools of both sexes looked calmly on, offering not the least resistance when their cattle and provisions were being taken from them. On the contrary, they invited the soldiers to come and live with them, saying: "If you, dear friends, find it is difficult to earn a living in your own land, come and live with us, where everything is plentiful."

The soldiers decided to remain, finding the people happy and prosperous, with enough surplus food to supply many of their neighbors. They were surprised at the cordial greetings which they everywhere received, and, returning to the ruler of Tarakania, they said: "We cannot fight with these people – take us to another place. We would much prefer the dangers of actual warfare to this unsoldierly method of subduing the village."

The Tarakanian ruler, becoming enraged, ordered the soldiers to destroy the whole kingdom, plunder the villages, burn the houses and provisions, and slaughter the cattle.

"Should you disobey my orders," said he, "I will have every one of you executed."

The soldiers, becoming frightened, started to do as they were ordered, but the fools wept bitterly, offering no resistance, men, women, and children all joining in the general lamentation.

"Why do you treat us so cruelly?" they cried to the invading soldiers. "Why do you wish to destroy everything we have? If you have more need of these things than we have, why not take them with you and leave us in peace?"

The soldiers, becoming saddened with remorse, refused further to pursue their path of destruction – the entire army scattering in many directions.

# CHAPTER XII

The old devil, failing to ruin Ivan's kingdom with soldiers, transformed himself into a nobleman, dressed exquisitely, and became one of Ivan's subjects, with the intention of compassing the downfall of his kingdom – as he had done with that of Tarras.

The "nobleman" said to Ivan: "I desire to teach you wisdom and to render you other service. I will build you a palace and factories."

"Very well," said Ivan; "you may live with us."

The next day the "nobleman" appeared on the Square with a sack of gold in his hand and a plan for building a house, saying to the people: "You are living like pigs, and I am going to teach you how to live decently. You are to build a house for me according to this plan. I will superintend the work myself, and will pay you for your services in gold," showing them at the same time the contents of his sack.

The fools were amused. They had never before seen any money. Their business was conducted entirely by exchange of farm products or by hiring themselves out to work by the day in return for whatever they most needed. They therefore glanced at the gold pieces with amazement, and said, "What nice toys they would be to play with!" In return for the gold they gave their services and brought the "nobleman" the produce of their farms.

The old devil was overjoyed as he thought, "Now my enterprise is on a fair road and I will be able to ruin the Fool – as I did his brothers."

The fools obtained sufficient gold to distribute among the entire community, the women and young girls of the village wearing much of it as ornaments, while to the children they gave some pieces to play with on the streets.

When they had secured all they wanted they stopped working and the "noblemen" did not get his house more than half finished. He had neither provisions nor cattle for the year, and ordered the people to bring him both. He directed them also to go on with the building of the palace and factories. He promised to pay them liberally in gold for everything they did. No one responded to his call – only once in awhile a little boy or girl would call to exchange eggs for his gold.

Thus was the "nobleman" deserted, and, having nothing to eat, he went to the village to procure some provisions for his dinner. He went to one house and offered gold in return for a chicken, but was refused, the owner saying: "We have enough of that already and do not want any more."

He next went to a fish-woman to buy some herring, when she, too, refused to accept his gold in return for fish, saying: "I do not wish it, my dear man; I have no children to whom I can give it to play with. I have three pieces which I keep as curiosities only."

He then went to a peasant to buy bread, but he also refused to accept the gold. "I have no use for it," said he, "unless you wish to give it for Christ's sake; then it will be a different matter, and I will tell my baba[9] to cut a piece of bread for you."

The old devil was so angry that he ran away from the peasant, spitting and cursing as he went.

Not only did the offer to accept in the name of Christ anger him, but the very mention of the name was like the thrust of a knife in his throat.

The old devil did not succeed in getting any bread, and in his efforts to secure other articles of food he met with the same failure. The people had all the gold they wanted and what pieces they had they regarded as curiosities. They said to the old devil: "If you bring us something

---

9  old woman

else in exchange for food, or come to ask for Christ's sake, we will give you all you want."

But the old devil had nothing but gold, and was too lazy to work; and being unable to accept anything for Christ's sake, he was greatly enraged.

"What else do you want?" he said. "I will give you gold with which you can buy everything you want, and you need labor no longer."

But the fools would not accept his gold, nor listen to him. Thus the old devil was obliged to go to sleep hungry.

Tidings of this condition of affairs soon reached the ears of Ivan. The people went to him and said: "What shell we do? This nobleman appeared among us; he is well dressed; he wishes to eat and drink of the best, but is unwilling to work, and does not beg for food for Christ's sake. He only offers every one gold pieces. At first we gave him everything he wanted, taking the gold pieces in exchange just as curiosities; but now we have enough of them and refuse to accept any more from him. What shall we do with him? he may die of hunger!"

Ivan heard all they had to say, and told them to employ him as a shepherd, taking turns in doing so.

The old devil saw no other way out of the difficulty and was obliged to submit.

It soon came the old devil's turn to go to Ivan's house. He went there to dinner and found Ivan's dumb sister preparing the meal. She was often cheated by the lazy people, who while they did not work, yet ate up all the gruel. But she learned to know the lazy people from the condition of their hands. Those with great welts on their hands she invited first to the table, and those having smooth white hands had to take what was left.

The old devil took a seat at the table, but the dumb girl, taking his hands, looked at them, and seeing them white and clean, and with long nails, swore at him and put him from the table.

Ivan's wife said to the old devil: "You must excuse my sister-in-law; she will not allow any one to sit at the table whose hands have not been hardened by toil, so you will have to wait until the dinner is over and then you can have what is left. With it you must be satisfied."

The old devil was very much offended that he was made to eat with "pigs," as he expressed it, and complained to Ivan, saying: "The foolish law you have in your kingdom, that all persons must work, is surely the invention of fools. People who work for a living are not always forced to labor with their hands. Do you think wise men labor so?"

Ivan replied: "Well, what do fools know about it? We all work with our hands."

"And for that reason you are fools," replied the devil. "I can teach you how to use your brains, and you will find such labor more beneficial."

Ivan was surprised at hearing this, and said:

"Well, it is perhaps not without good reason that we are called fools."

"It is not so easy to work with the brain," the old devil said. "You will not give me anything to eat because my hands have not the appearance of being toil-hardened, but you must understand that it is much harder to do brain-work, and sometimes the head feels like bursting with the effort it is forced to make."

"Then why do you not select some light work that you can perform with your hands?" Ivan asked.

The devil said: "I torment myself with brain-work because I have pity for you fools, for, if I did not torture myself, people like you would remain fools for all eternity. I have exercised my brain a great deal during my life, and now I am able to teach you."

Ivan was greatly surprised and said: "Very well; teach us, so that when our hands are tired we can use our heads to replace them."

The devil promised to instruct the people, and Ivan announced the fact throughout his kingdom.

The devil was willing to teach all those who came to him how to use the head instead of the hands, so as to produce more with the former than with the latter.

In Ivan's kingdom there was a high tower, which was reached by a long, narrow ladder leading up to the balcony, and Ivan told the old devil that from the top of the tower every one could see him.

So the old devil went up to the balcony and addressed the people.

The fools came in great crowds to hear what the old devil had to say, thinking that he really meant to tell them how to work with the head. But the old devil only told them in words what to do, and did not give them any practical instruction. He said that men working only with their hands could not make a living. The fools did not understand what he said to them and looked at him in amazement, and then departed for their daily work.

The old devil addressed them for two days from the balcony, and at the end of that time, feeling hungry, he asked the people to bring him some bread. But they only laughed at him and told him if he could work better with his head than with his hands he could also find bread for himself. He addressed the people for yet another day, and they went to hear him from curiosity, but soon left him to return to their work.

Ivan asked, "Well, did the nobleman work with his head?"

"Not yet," they said; "so far he has only talked."

One day, while the old devil was standing on the balcony, he became weak, and, falling down, hurt his head against a pole.

Seeing this, one of the fools ran to Ivan's wife and said, "The gentleman has at last commenced to work with his head."

She ran to the field to tell Ivan, who was much surprised, and said, "Let us go and see him."

He turned his horses' heads in the direction of the tower, where the old devil remained weak from hunger and was still suspended from the pole, with his body swaying back and forth and his head striking the lower part of the pole each time it came in contact with it. While Ivan was looking, the old devil started down the steps head-first – as they supposed, to count them.

"Well," said Ivan, "he told the truth after all – that sometimes from this kind of work the head bursts. This is far worse than welts on the hands."

The old devil fell to the ground head-foremost. Ivan approached him, but at that instant the ground opened and the devil disappeared, leaving only a hole to show where he had gone.

Ivan scratched his head and said: "See here; such nastiness! This is yet another devil. He looks like the father of the little ones."

Ivan still lives, and people flock to his kingdom. His brothers come to him and he feeds them.

To every one who comes to him and says, "Give us food," he replies: "Very well; you are welcome. We have plenty of everything."

There is only one unchangeable custom observed in Ivan's kingdom: The man with toil-hardened hands is always given a seat at the table, while the possessor of soft white hands must be contented with what is left.

# STORY 3

## A LOST OPPORTUNITY

\*\*\*

"Then came Peter to Him, and said,
Lord, how oft shall my brother
sin against me, and I forgive him? till
seven times?"...
"So likewise shall My heavenly Father
do also unto you, if ye
from your hearts forgive not every one
his brother their
trespasses."
ST. MATTHEW

In a certain village there lived a peasant by the name of Ivan Scherbakoff. He was prosperous, strong, and vigorous, and was considered the hardest worker in the whole village. He had three sons, who supported themselves by their own labor. The eldest was married, the second about to be married, and the youngest took care of the horses and occasionally attended to the plowing.

The peasant's wife, Ivanovna, was intelligent and industrious, while her daughter-in-law was a simple, quiet soul, but a hard worker.

There was only one idle person in the household, and that was Ivan's father, a very old man who for seven years had suffered from asthma, and who spent the greater part of his time lying on the brick oven.

Ivan had plenty of everything – three horses, with one colt, a cow with calf, and fifteen sheep. The women made the men's clothes, and in addition to performing all the necessary household labor, also worked in the field; while the men's industry was confined altogether to the farm.

What was left of the previous year's supply of provisions was ample for their needs, and they sold a quantity of oats sufficient to pay their taxes and other expenses.

Thus life went smoothly for Ivan.

The peasant's next-door neighbor was a son of Gordey Ivanoff, called "Gavryl the Lame." It once happened that Ivan had a quarrel with him; but while old man Gordey was yet alive, and Ivan's father was the head of the household, the two peasants lived as good neighbors should. If the women of one house required the use of a sieve or pail, they borrowed it from the inmates of the other house. The same condition of affairs existed between the men. They lived more like one family, the one dividing his possessions with the other, and perfect harmony reigned between the two families.

If a stray calf or cow invaded the garden of one of the farmers, the other willingly drove it away, saying: "Be careful, neighbor, that your stock does not again stray into my garden; we should put a fence up." In the same way they had no secrets from each other. The doors of their houses and barns had neither bolts nor locks, so sure were they of each other's honesty. Not a shadow of suspicion darkened their daily intercourse.

Thus lived the old people.

In time the younger members of the two households started farming. It soon became apparent that they would not get along as peacefully as the old people had done, for they began quarrelling without the slightest provocation.

A hen belonging to Ivan's daughter-in-law commenced laying eggs, which the young woman collected each morning, intending to keep them for the Easter holidays. She made daily visits to the barn, where, under an old wagon, she was sure to find the precious egg.

One day the children frightened the hen and she flew over their neighbor's fence and laid her egg in their garden.

Ivan's daughter-in-law heard the hen cackling, but said: "I am very busy just at present, for this is the eve of a holy day, and I must clean and arrange this room. I will go for the egg later on."

When evening came, and she had finished her task, she went to the barn, and as usual looked under the old wagon, expecting to find an egg. But, alas! no egg was visible in the accustomed place.

Greatly disappointed, she returned to the house and inquired of her mother-in-law and the other members of the family if they had taken it. "No," they said, "we know nothing of it."

Taraska, the youngest brother-in-law, coming in soon after, she also inquired of him if he knew anything about the missing egg. "Yes," he replied; "your pretty, crested hen laid her egg in our neighbors' garden, and after she had finished cackling she flew back again over the fence."

The young woman, greatly surprised on hearing this, turned and looked long and seriously at the hen, which was sitting with closed eyes beside the rooster in the chimney-corner. She asked the hen where it laid the egg. At the sound of her voice it simply opened and closed its eyes, but could make no answer.

She then went to the neighbors' house, where she was met by an old woman, who said: "What do you want, young woman?"

Ivan's daughter-in-law replied: "You see, babushka,[10] my hen flew into your yard this morning. Did she not lay an egg there?"

"We did not see any," the old woman replied; "we have our own hens – God be praised! – and they have been laying for this long time. We hunt only for the eggs our own hens lay, and have no use for the eggs other people's hens lay. Another thing I want to tell you, young woman: we do not go into other people's yards to look for eggs."

Now this speech greatly angered the young woman, and she replied in the same spirit in which she had been spoken to, only using much stronger language and speaking at greater length.

---

10 grandmother

The neighbor replied in the same angry manner, and finally the women began to abuse each other and call vile names. It happened that old Ivan's wife, on her way to the well for water, heard the dispute, and joined the others, taking her daughter-in-law's part.

Gavryl's housekeeper, hearing the noise, could not resist the temptation to join the rest and to make her voice heard. As soon as she appeared on the scene, she, too, began to abuse her neighbor, reminding her of many disagreeable things which had happened (and many which had not happened) between them. She became so infuriated during her denunciations that she lost all control of herself, and ran around like some mad creature.

Then all the women began to shout at the same time, each trying to say two words to another's one, and using the vilest language in the quarreller's vocabulary.

"You are such and such," shouted one of the women. "You are a thief, a schlukha;[11] your father-in-law is even now starving, and you have no shame. You beggar, you borrowed my sieve and broke it. You made a large hole in it, and did not buy me another."

"You have our scale-beam," cried another woman, "and must give it back to me;" whereupon she seized the scale-beam and tried to remove it from the shoulders of Ivan's wife.

In the melee which followed they upset the pails of water. They tore the covering from each other's head, and a general fight ensued.

Gavryl's wife had by this time joined in the fracas, and he, crossing the field and seeing the trouble, came to her rescue.

Ivan and his son, seeing that their womenfolk were being badly used,

---

[11] a mean, dirty, low creature

jumped into the midst of the fray, and a fearful fight followed.

Ivan was the most powerful peasant in all the country round, and it did not take him long to disperse the crowd, for they flew in all directions. During the progress of the fight Ivan tore out a large quantity of Gavryl's beard.

By this time a large crowd of peasants had collected, and it was with the greatest difficulty that they persuaded the two families to stop quarrelling.

This was the beginning.

Gavryl took the portion of his beard which Ivan had torn out, and, wrapping it in a paper, went to the volostnoye (moujiks' court) and entered a complaint against Ivan.

Holding up the hair, he said, "I did not grow this for that bear Ivan to tear out!"

Gavryl's wife went round among the neighbors, telling them that they must not repeat what she told them, but that she and her husband were going to get the best of Ivan, and that he was to be sent to Siberia.

And so the quarrelling went on.

The poor old grandfather, sick with asthma and lying on the brick oven all the time, tried from the first to dissuade them from quarrelling, and begged of them to live in peace; but they would not listen to his good advice. He said to them: "You children are making a great fuss and much trouble about nothing. I beg of you to stop and think of what a little thing has caused all this trouble. It has arisen from only one egg. If our neighbors' children picked it up, it is all right. God bless them! One egg is of but little value, and without it God will supply sufficient for all our needs."

Ivan's daughter-in-law here interposed and said, "But they called us vile names."

The old grandfather again spoke, saying: "Well, even if they did call you bad names, it would have been better to return good for evil, and by your example show them how to speak better. Such conduct on your part would have been best for all concerned." He continued: "Well, you had a fight, you wicked people. Such things sometimes happen, but it would be better if you went afterward and asked forgiveness and buried your grievances out of sight. Scatter them to the four winds of heaven, for if you do not do so it will be the worse for you in the end."

The younger members of the family, still obstinate, refused to profit by the old man's advice, and declared he was not right, and that he only liked to grumble in his old-fashioned way.

Ivan refused to go to his neighbor, as the grandfather wished, saying: "I did not tear out Gavryl's beard. He did it himself, and his son tore my shirt and trousers into shreds."

Ivan entered suit against Gavryl. He first went to the village justice, and not getting satisfaction from him he carried his case to the village court.

While the neighbors were wrangling over the affair, each suing the other, it happened that a perch-bolt from Gavryl's wagon was lost; and the women of Gavryl's household accused Ivan's son of stealing it.

They said: "We saw him in the night-time pass by our window, on his way to where the wagon was standing." "And my kumushka,"[12] said one of them, "told me that Ivan's son had offered it for sale at the kabak."[13]

This accusation caused them again to go into court for a settlement of their grievances.

While the heads of the families were trying to have their troubles settled in court, their home quarrels were constant,

---

[12] sponsor

[13] tavern

and frequently resulted in hand-to-hand encounters. Even the little children followed the example of their elders and quarrelled incessantly.

The women, when they met on the riverbank to do the family washing, instead of attending to their work passed the time in abusing each other, and not infrequently they came to blows.

At first the male members of the families were content with accusing each other of various crimes, such as stealing and like meannesses. But the trouble in this mild form did not last long.

They soon resorted to other measures. They began to appropriate one another's things without asking permission, while various articles disappeared from both houses and could not be found. This was done out of revenge.

This example being set by the men, the women and children also followed, and life soon became a burden to all who took part in the strife.

Ivan Scherbakoff and "Gavryl the Lame" at last laid their trouble before the mir (village meeting), in addition to having been in court and calling on the justice of the peace. Both of the latter had grown tired of them and their incessant wrangling. One time Gavryl would succeed in having Ivan fined, and if he was not able to pay it he would be locked up in the cold dreary prison for days. Then it would be Ivan's turn to get Gavryl punished in like manner, and the greater the injury the one could do the other the more delight he took in it.

The success of either in having the other punished only served to increase their rage against each other, until they were like mad dogs in their warfare.

If anything went wrong with one of them he immediately accused his adversary of conspiring to ruin him, and sought revenge without stopping to inquire into the rights of the case.

When the peasants went into court, and had each other fined and imprisoned, it did not soften their hearts in the least. They would only taunt one another on such occasions, saying: "Never mind; I will repay you for all this."

This state of affairs lasted for six years.

Ivan's father, the sick old man, constantly repeated his good advice. He would try to arouse their conscience by saying: "What are you doing, my children? Can you not throw off all these troubles, pay more attention to your business, and suppress your anger against your neighbors? There is no use in your continuing to live in this way, for the more enraged you become against each other the worse it is for you."

Again was the wise advice of the old man rejected.

At the beginning of the seventh year of the existence of the feud it happened that a daughter-in-law of Ivan's was present at a marriage. At the wedding feast she openly accused Gavryl of stealing a horse. Gavryl was intoxicated at the time and was in no mood to stand the insult, so in retaliation he struck the woman a terrific blow, which confined her to her bed for more than a week. The woman being in delicate health, the worst results were feared.

Ivan, glad of a fresh opportunity to harass his neighbor, lodged a formal complaint before the district-attorney, hoping to rid himself forever of Gavryl by having him sent to Siberia.

On examining the complaint the district-attorney would not consider it, as by that time the injured woman was walking about and as well as ever.

Thus again Ivan was disappointed in obtaining his revenge, and, not being satisfied with the district-attorney's decision, had the case transferred to the court, where he used all possible means to push his suit. To secure the favor of the starshina (village mayor) he made him a present of half a gallon of sweet vodki; and to the mayor's pisar (secretary) also he gave presents. By this means he succeeded in securing a verdict against Gavryl. The sentence was that Gavryl was to receive twenty lashes on his bare back, and the punishment was to be administered in the yard which surrounded the court-house.

When Ivan heard the sentence read he looked triumphantly at Gavryl to see what effect it would produce on him. Gavryl turned very white on hearing that he was to be treated with such indignity, and turning his back on the assembly left the room without uttering a word.

Ivan followed him out, and as he reached his horse he heard Gavryl saying: "Very well; my spine will burn from the lashes, but something will burn with greater fierceness in Ivan's household before long."

Ivan, on hearing these words, instantly returned to the court, and going up to the judges said: "Oh! just judges, he threatens to burn my house and all it contains."

A messenger was immediately sent in search of Gavryl, who was soon found and again brought into the presence of the judges.

"Is it true," they asked, "that you said you would burn Ivan's house and all it contained?"

Gavryl replied: "I did not say anything of the kind. You may give me as many lashes as you please – that is, if you have the power to do so. It seems to me that I alone have to suffer for the truth, while he," pointing to Ivan, "is allowed to do and say what he pleases." Gavryl wished to say something more, but his lips trembled, and the words refused to come; so in silence he turned his face toward the wall.

The sight of so much suffering moved even the judges to pity, and, becoming alarmed at Gavryl's continued silence, they said, "He may do both his neighbor and himself some frightful injury."

"See here, my brothers," said one feeble old judge, looking at Ivan and Gavryl as he spoke, "I think you had better try to arrange this matter peaceably. You, brother Gavryl, did wrong to strike a woman who was in delicate health. It was a lucky thing for you that God had mercy on you and that the woman did not die, for if she had I know not what dire misfortune might have overtaken you! It will not do either of you any good to go on living as you are at present. Go, Gavryl, and make friends with Ivan; I am sure he will forgive you, and we will set aside the verdict just given."

The secretary on hearing this said: "It is impossible to do this on the present case. According to Article 117 this matter has gone too far to be settled peaceably now, as the verdict has been rendered and must be enforced."

But the judges would not listen to the secretary, saying to him: "You talk altogether too much. You must remember that the first thing is to fulfill God's command to 'Love thy neighbor as thyself,' and all will be well with you."

Thus with kind words the judges tried to reconcile the two peasants. Their words fell on stony ground, however, for Gavryl would not listen to them.

"I am fifty years old," said Gavryl, "and have a son married, and never from my birth has the lash been applied to my back; but now this bear Ivan has secured a verdict against me which condemns me to receive twenty lashes, and I am forced to bow to this decision and suffer the shame of a public beating. Well, he will have cause to remember this."

At this Gavryl's voice trembled and he stopped speaking, and turning his back on the judges took his departure.

It was about ten versts' distance from the court to the homes of the neighbors, and this Ivan travelled late. The women had already gone out for the cattle. He unharnessed his horse and put everything in its place, and then went into the izba (room), but found no one there.

The men had not yet returned from their work in the field and the women had gone to look for the cattle, so that all about the place was quiet. Going into the room, Ivan seated himself on a wooden bench and soon became lost in thought. He remembered how, when Gavryl first heard the sentence which had been passed upon him, he grew very pale, and turned his face to the wall, all the while remaining silent.

Ivan's heart ached when he thought of the disgrace which he had been the means of bringing upon Gavryl, and he wondered how he would feel if the same sentence had been passed upon him. His thoughts were interrupted by the coughing of his father, who was lying on the oven.

The old man, on seeing Ivan, came down off the oven, and slowly approaching his son seated himself on the bench beside him, looking at him as though ashamed.

He continued to cough as he leaned on the table and said, "Well, did they sentence him?"

"Yes, they sentenced him to receive twenty lashes," replied Ivan.

On hearing this the old man sorrowfully shook his head, and said: "This is very bad, Ivan, and what is the meaning of it all? It is indeed very bad, but not so bad for Gavryl as for yourself. Well, suppose his sentence IS carried out, and he gets the twenty lashes, what will it benefit you?"

"He will not again strike a woman," Ivan replied.

"What is it he will not do? He does not do anything worse than what you are constantly doing!"

This conversation enraged Ivan, and he shouted: "Well, what did he do? He beat a woman nearly to death, and even now he threatens to burn my house! Must I bow to him for all this?"

The old man sighed deeply as he said: "You, Ivan, are strong and free to go wherever you please, while I have been lying for years on the oven. You think that you know everything and that I do not know anything. No! you are still a child, and as such you cannot see that a kind of madness controls your actions and blinds your sight. The sins of others are ever before you, while you resolutely keep your own behind your back. I know that what Gavryl did was wrong, but if he alone should do wrong there would be no evil in the world. Do you think that all the evil in the world is the work of one man alone? No! it requires two persons to work much evil in the world. You see only the bad in Gavryl's character, but you are blind to the evil that is in your own nature. If he alone were bad and you good, then there would be no wrong."

The old man, after a pause, continued: "Who tore Gavryl's beard? Who destroyed his heaps of rye? Who dragged him into court? — and yet you try to put all the blame on his shoulders. You are behaving very badly yourself, and for that reason you are wrong. I did not act in such a manner, and certainly I never taught you to do so. I lived in peace with Gavryl's father all the time we were neighbors. We were always the best of friends. If he was without flour his wife would come to me and say, 'Diadia Frol,[14] we need flour.' I would then say: 'My good woman, go to the warehouse and take as much as you want.' If he had no one to care for his horses I would say, 'Go, Ivanushka,[15] and help him to care for them.' If I required anything I would go to him and say, 'Grandfather Gordey, I need this or that,' and he would always reply, 'Take just whatever you want.' By this means we passed an easy and peaceful life. But what is your life compared with it? As the soldiers fought at Plevna, so are you and Gavryl fighting all the time, only that your battles are far more disgraceful than that fought at Plevna."

---

[14] Grandfather

[15] diminutive of Ivan

The old man went on: "And you call this living! and what a sin it all is! You are a peasant, and the head of the house; therefore, the responsibility of the trouble rests with you. What an example you set your wife and children by constantly quarrelling with your neighbor! Only a short time since your little boy, Taraska, was cursing his aunt Arina, and his mother only laughed at it, saying, 'What a bright child he is!' Is that right? You are to blame for all this. You should think of the salvation of your soul. Is that the way to do it? You say one unkind word to me and I will reply with two. You will give me one slap in the face, and I will retaliate with two slaps. No, my son; Christ did not teach us foolish people to act in such a way. If any one should say an unkind word to you it is better not to answer at all; but if you do reply do it kindly, and his conscience will accuse him, and he will regret his unkindness to you. This is the way Christ taught us to live. He tells us that if a person smite us on the one cheek we should offer unto him the other. That is Christ's command to us, and we should follow it. You should therefore subdue your pride. Am I not right?"

Ivan remained silent, but his father's words had sunk deep into his heart.

The old man coughed and continued: "Do you think Christ thought us wicked? Did he not die that we might be saved? Now you think only of this earthly life. Are you better or worse for thinking alone of it? Are you better or worse for having begun that Plevna battle? Think of your expense at court and the time lost in going back and forth, and what have you gained? Your sons have reached manhood, and are able now to work for you. You are therefore at liberty to enjoy life and be happy. With the assistance of your children you could reach a high state of prosperity. But now your property instead of increasing is gradually growing less, and why? It is the result of your pride. When it becomes necessary for you and your boys to go to the field to work, your enemy instead summons you to appear at court or before some kind of judicial person. If you do not plow at the proper time and sow at the proper time mother earth will not yield up her products, and you and your children will be left destitute. Why did your oats fail this year? When did you sow them? Were you not quarrelling with your neighbor instead of attending to your work? You have just now returned from the town, where you have been the means of having your neighbor humiliated. You have succeeded in getting him sentenced, but in the end the punishment will fall on your own shoulders. Oh! my child, it would be better for you to attend to your work on the farm and train your boys to become good farmers and honest men. If any one offend you forgive him for Christ's sake, and then prosperity will smile on your work and a light and happy feeling will fill your heart."

Ivan still remained silent.

The old father in a pleading voice continued: "Take an old man's advice. Go and harness your horse, drive back to the court, and withdraw all these complaints against your neighbor. To-morrow go to him, offer to make peace in Christ's name, and invite him to your house. It will be a holy day (the birth of the Virgin Mary). Get out the samovar and have some vodki, and over both forgive and forget each other's sins, promising not to transgress in the future, and advise your women and children to do the same."

Ivan heaved a deep sigh but felt easier in his heart, as he thought: "The old man speaks the truth;" yet he was in doubt as to how he would put his father's advice into practice.

The old man, surmising his uncertainty, said to Ivan: "Go, Ivanushka; do not delay. Extinguish the fire in the beginning, before it grows large, for then it may be impossible."

Ivan's father wished to say more to him, but was prevented by the arrival of the women, who came into the room chattering like so many magpies. They had already heard of Gavryl's sentence, and of how he threatened to set fire to Ivan's house. They found out all about it, and in telling it to their neighbors added their own versions of the story, with the usual exaggeration. Meeting in the pasture-ground, they proceeded to quarrel with Gavryl's women. They related how the latter's daughter-in-law had threatened to secure the influence of the manager of a certain noble's estate in behalf of his friend Gavryl; also that the school-teacher was writing a petition to the Czar himself against Ivan, explaining in detail his theft of the perchbolt and partial destruction of Gavryl's garden – declaring that half of Ivan's land was to be given to them.

Ivan listened calmly to their stories, but his anger was soon aroused once more, when he abandoned his intention of making peace with Gavryl.

As Ivan was always busy about the household, he did not stop to speak to the wrangling women, but immediately left the room, directing his steps toward the barn. Before getting through with his work the sun had set and the boys had returned from their plowing. Ivan met them and asked about their work, helping them to put things in order and leaving the broken horse-collar aside to be repaired. He intended to perform some other duties, but it became too dark and he was obliged to leave them till the next day. He fed the cattle, however, and opened the gate that Taraska might take his horses to pasture for the night, after which he closed it again and went into the house for his supper.

By this time he had forgotten all about Gavryl and what his father had said to him. Yet, just as he touched the door-knob, he heard sounds of quarrelling proceeding from his neighbor's house.

"What do I want with that devil?" shouted Gavryl to some one. "He deserves to be killed!"

Ivan stopped and listened for a moment, when he shook his head threateningly and entered the room. When he came in, the apartment was already lighted. His daughter-in-law was working with her loom, while the old woman was preparing the supper. The eldest son was twining strings for his lapti (peasant's shoes made of strips of bark from the linden-tree). The other son was sitting by the table reading a book. The room presented a pleasant appearance, everything being in order and the inmates apparently gay and happy – the only dark shadow being that cast over the household by Ivan's trouble with his neighbor.

Ivan came in very cross, and, angrily throwing aside a cat which lay sleeping on the bench, cursed the women for having misplaced a pail. He looked very sad and serious, and, seating himself in a corner of the room, proceeded to repair the horse-collar. He could not forget Gavryl, however – the threatening words he had used in the court-room and those which Ivan had just heard.

Presently Taraska came in, and after having his supper, put on his sheepskin coat, and, taking some bread with him, returned to watch over his horses for the night. His eldest brother wished to accompany him, but Ivan himself arose and went with him as far as the porch.

The night was dark and cloudy and a strong wind was blowing, which produced a peculiar whistling sound that was most unpleasant to the ear. Ivan helped his son to mount his horse, which, followed by a colt, started off on a gallop.

Ivan stood for a few moments looking around him and listening to the clatter of the horse's hoofs as Taraska rode down the village street. He heard him meet other boys on horseback, who rode quite as well as Taraska, and soon all were lost in the darkness.

Ivan remained standing by the gate in a gloomy mood, as he was unable to banish from his mind the harassing thoughts of Gavryl, which the latter's menacing words had inspired: "Something will burn with greater fierceness in Ivan's household before long."

"He is so desperate," thought Ivan, "that he may set fire to my house regardless of the danger to his own. At present everything is dry, and as the wind is so high he may sneak from the back of his own building, start a fire, and get away unseen by any of us.

"He may burn and steal without being found out, and thus go unpunished. I wish I could catch him."

This thought so worried Ivan that he decided not to return to his house, but went out and stood on the street-corner.

"I guess," thought Ivan to himself, "I will take a walk around the premises and examine everything carefully, for who knows what he may be tempted to do?"

Ivan moved very cautiously round to the back of his buildings, not making the slightest noise, and scarcely daring to breathe. Just as he reached a corner of the house he looked toward the fence, and it seemed to him that he saw something moving, and that it was slowly creeping toward the corner of the house opposite to where he was standing. He stepped back quickly and hid himself in the shadow of the building. Ivan stood and listened, but all was quiet. Not a sound could be heard but the moaning of the wind through the branches of the trees, and the rustling of the leaves as it caught them up and whirled them in all directions. So dense was the darkness that it was at first impossible for Ivan to see more than a few feet beyond where he stood.

After a time, however, his sight becoming accustomed to the gloom, he was enabled to see for a considerable distance. The plow and his other farming implements stood just where he had placed them. He could see also the opposite corner of the house.

He looked in every direction, but no one was in sight, and he thought to himself that his imagination must have played him some trick, leading him to believe that some one was moving when there really was no one there.

Still, Ivan was not satisfied, and decided to make a further examination of the premises. As on the previous occasion, he moved so very cautiously that he could not hear even the sound of his own footsteps. He had taken the precaution to remove his shoes, that he might step the more noiselessly. When he reached the corner of the barn it again seemed to him that he saw something moving, this time near the plow; but it quickly disappeared. By this time Ivan's heart was beating very fast, and he was standing in a listening attitude when a sudden flash of light illumined the spot, and he could distinctly see the figure of a man seated on his haunches with his back turned toward him, and in the act of lighting a bunch of straw which he held in his hand! Ivan's heart began to beat yet faster, and he became terribly excited, walking up and down with rapid strides, but without making a noise.

Ivan said: "Well, now, he cannot get away, for he will be caught in the very act."

Ivan had taken a few more steps when suddenly a bright light flamed up, but not in the same spot in which he had seen the figure of the man sitting. Gavryl had lighted the straw, and running to the barn held it under the edge of the roof, which began to burn fiercely; and by the light of the fire he could distinctly see his neighbor standing.

As an eagle springs at a skylark, so sprang Ivan at Gavryl, saying: "I will tear you into pieces! You shall not get away from me this time!"

But "Gavryl the Lame," hearing footsteps, wrenched himself free from Ivan's grasp and ran like a hare past the buildings.

Ivan, now terribly excited, shouted, "You shall not escape me!" and started in pursuit; but just as he reached him and was about to grasp the collar of his coat, Gavryl succeeded in jumping to one side, and Ivan's coat became entangled in something and he was thrown violently to the ground. Jumping quickly to his feet he shouted, "Karaool! derji!"(watch! catch!)

While Ivan was regaining his feet Gavryl succeeded in reaching his house, but Ivan followed so quickly that he caught up with him before he could enter. Just as he was about to grasp him he was struck on the head with some hard substance. He had been hit on the temple as with a stone. The blow was struck by Gavryl, who had picked up an oaken stave, and with it gave Ivan a terrible blow on the head.

Ivan was stunned, and bright sparks danced before his eyes, while he swayed from side to side like a drunken man, until finally all became dark and he sank to the ground unconscious.

When he recovered his senses, Gavryl was nowhere to be seen, but all around him was as light as day. Strange sounds proceeded from the direction of his house, and turning his face that way he saw that his barns were on fire. The rear parts of both were already destroyed, and the flames were leaping toward the front. Fire, smoke, and bits of burning straw were being rapidly whirled by the high wind over to where his house stood, and he expected every moment to see it burst into flames.

"What is this, brother?" Ivan cried out, as he beat his thighs with his hands. "I should have stopped to snatch the bunch of burning straw, and, throwing it on the ground, should have extinguished it with my feet!"

Ivan tried to cry out and arouse his people, but his lips refused to utter a word. He next tried to run, but he could not move his feet, and his legs seemed to twist themselves around each other. After several attempts he succeeded in taking one or two steps, when he again began to stagger and gasp for breath. It was some moments before he made another attempt to move, but after considerable exertion he finally reached the barn, the rear of which was by this time entirely consumed; and the corner of his house had already caught fire. Dense volumes of smoke began to pour out of the room, which made it difficult to approach.

A crowd of peasants had by this time gathered, but they found it impossible to save their homes, so they carried everything which they could to a place of safety. The cattle they drove into neighboring pastures and left some one to care for them.

The wind carried the sparks from Ivan's house to Gavryl's, and it, too, took fire and was consumed. The wind continued to increase with great fury, and the flames spread to both sides of the street, until in a very short time more than half the village was burned.

The members of Ivan's household had great difficulty in getting out of the burning building, but the neighbors rescued the old man and carried him to a place of safety, while the women escaped in only their night-clothes. Everything was burned, including the cattle and all the farm implements. The women lost their trunks, which were filled with quantities of clothing, the accumulation of years. The storehouse and all the provisions perished in the flames, not even the chickens being saved.

Gavryl, however, more fortunate than Ivan, saved his cattle and a few other things.

The village was burning all night.

Ivan stood near his home, gazing sadly at the burning building, and he kept constantly repeating to himself: "I should have taken away the bunch of burning straw, and have stamped out the fire with my feet."

But when he saw his home fall in a smouldering heap, in spite of the terrible heat he sprang into the midst of it and carried out a charred log. The women seeing him, and fearing that he would lose his life, called to him to come back, but he would not pay any attention to them and went a second time to get a log. Still weak from the terrible blow which Gavryl had given him, he was overcome by the heat, and fell into the midst of the burning mass. Fortunately, his eldest son saw him fall, and rushing into the fire succeeded in getting hold of him and carrying him out of it. Ivan's hair, beard, and clothing were burned entirely off. His hands were also frightfully injured, but he seemed indifferent to pain.

"Grief drove him crazy," the people said.

The fire was growing less, but Ivan still stood where he could see it, and kept repeating to himself, "I should have taken," etc.

The morning after the fire the starosta (village elder) sent his son to Ivan to tell him that the old man, his father, was dying, and wanted to see him to bid him good-bye.

In his grief Ivan had forgotten all about his father, and could not understand what was being said to him. In a dazed way he asked: "What father? Whom does he want?"

The elder's son again repeated his father's message to Ivan. "Your aged parent is at our house dying, and he wants to see you and bid you good-bye. Won't you go now, uncle Ivan?" the boy said.

Finally Ivan understood, and followed the elder's son.

When Ivan's father was carried from the oven, he was slightly injured by a big bunch of burning straw falling on him just as he reached the street. To insure his safety he was removed to the elder's house, which stood a considerable distance from his late home, and where it was not likely that the fire would reach it.

When Ivan arrived at the elder's home he found only the latter's wife and children, who were all seated on the brick oven. The old man was lying on a bench holding a lighted candle in his hand (a Russian custom when a person is dying). Hearing a noise, he turned his face toward the door, and when he saw it was his son he tried to move. He motioned for Ivan to come nearer, and when he did so he whispered in a trembling voice: "Well, Ivanushka, did I not tell you before what would be the result of this sad affair? Who set the village on fire?"

"He, he, batiushka;[16] he did it. I caught him. He placed the bunch of burning straw to the barn in my presence. Instead of running after him, I should have snatched the bunch of burning straw and throwing it on the ground have stamped it out with my feet; and then there would have been no fire."

"Ivan," said the old man, "death is fast approaching me, and remember that you also will have to die. Who did this dreadful thing? Whose is the sin?"

Ivan gazed at the noble face of his dying father and was silent. His heart was too full for utterance.

"In the presence of God," the old man continued, "whose is the sin?"

It was only now that the truth began to dawn upon Ivan's mind, and that he

---

16 little father

realized how foolish he had acted. He sobbed bitterly, and fell on his knees before his father, and, crying like a child, said:

"My dear father, forgive me, for Christ's sake, for I am guilty before God and before you!"

The old man transferred the lighted candle from his right hand to the left, and, raising the former to his forehead, tried to make the sign of the cross, but owing to weakness was unable to do so.

"Glory to Thee, O Lord! Glory to Thee!" he exclaimed; and turning his dim eyes toward his son, he said: "See here, Ivanushka! Ivanushka, my dear son!"

"What, my dear father?" Ivan asked.

"What are you going to do," replied the old man, "now that you have no home?"

Ivan cried and said: "I do not know how we shall live now."

The old man closed his eyes and made a movement with his lips, as if gathering his feeble strength for a final effort. Slowly opening his eyes, he whispered:

"Should you live according to God's commands you will be happy and prosperous again."

The old man was now silent for awhile and then, smiling sadly, he continued:

"See here, Ivanushka, keep silent concerning this trouble, and do not tell who set the village on fire. Forgive one sin of your neighbor's, and God will forgive two of yours."

Grasping the candle with both hands, Ivan's father heaved a deep sigh, and, stretching himself out on his back, yielded up the ghost.

\*\*\*

Ivan for once accepted his father's advice. He did not betray Gavryl, and no one ever learned the origin of the fire.

Ivan's heart became more kindly disposed toward his old enemy, feeling that much of the fault in connection with this sad affair rested with himself.

Gavryl was greatly surprised that Ivan did not denounce him before all the villagers, and at first he stood in much fear of him, but he soon afterward overcame this feeling.

The two peasants ceased to quarrel, and their families followed their example. While they were building new houses, both families lived beneath the same roof, and when they moved into their respective homes, Ivan and Gavryl lived on as good terms as their fathers had done before them.

Ivan remembered his dying father's command, and took deeply to heart the evident warning of God that A FIRE SHOULD BE EXTINGUISHED IN THE BEGINNING. If any one wronged him he did not seek revenge, but instead made every effort to settle the matter peaceably. If any one spoke to him unkindly, he did not answer in the same way, but replied softly, and tried to persuade the person not to speak evil. He taught the women and children of his household to do the same.

Ivan Scherbakoff was now a reformed man.

He lived well and peacefully, and again became prosperous.

Let us, therefore, have peace, live in brotherly love and kindness, and we will be happy.

# STORY 4

## "POLIKUSHKA;"

## The Lot of a Wicked Court Servant.

***

# CHAPTER I

Polikey was a court man – one of the staff of servants belonging to the court household of a boyarinia (lady of the nobility).

He held a very insignificant position on the estate, and lived in a rather poor, small house with his wife and children.

The house was built by the deceased nobleman whose widow he still continued to serve, and may be described as follows: The four walls surrounding the one izba (room) were built of stone, and the interior was ten yards square. A Russian stove stood in the centre, around which was a free passage. Each corner was fenced off as a separate inclosure to the extent of several feet, and the one nearest to the door (the smallest of all) was known as "Polikey's corner." Elsewhere in the room stood the bed (with quilt, sheet, and cotton pillows), the cradle (with a baby lying therein), and the three-legged table, on which the meals were prepared and the family washing was done. At the latter also Polikey was at work on the preparation of some materials for use in his profession – that of an amateur veterinary surgeon. A calf, some hens, the family clothes and household utensils, together with seven persons, filled the little home to the utmost of its capacity. It would indeed have been almost impossible for them to move around had it not been for the convenience of the stove, on which some of them slept at night, and which served as a table in the day-time.

It seemed hard to realize how so many persons managed to live in such close quarters.

Polikey's wife, Akulina, did the washing, spun and wove, bleached her linen, cooked and baked, and found time also to quarrel and gossip with her neighbors.

The monthly allowance of food which they received from the noblewoman's house was amply sufficient for the whole family, and there was always enough meal left to make mash for the cow. Their fuel they got free, and likewise the food for the cattle. In addition they were given a small piece of land on which to raise vegetables. They had a cow, a calf, and a number of chickens to care for.

Polikey was employed in the stables to take care of two stallions, and, when necessary, to bleed the horses and cattle and clean their hoofs.

In his treatment of the animals he used syringes, plasters, and various other remedies and appliances of his own invention. For these services he received whatever provisions were required by his family, and a certain sum of money – all of which would have been sufficient to enable them to live comfortably and even happily, if their hearts had not been filled with the shadow of a great sorrow.

This shadow darkened the lives of the entire family.

Polikey, while young, was employed in a horse-breeding establishment in a neighboring village. The head stableman was a notorious horse-thief, known far and wide as a great rogue, who, for his many misdeeds, was finally exiled to Siberia. Under his instruction Polikey underwent a course of training, and, being but a boy, was easily induced to perform many evil deeds. He became so expert in the various kinds of wickedness practiced by his teacher that, though he many times would gladly have abandoned his evil ways, he could not, owing to the great hold these early-formed habits had upon him. His father and mother died when he was but a child, and he had no one to point out to him the paths of virtue.

In addition to his other numerous shortcomings, Polikey was fond of strong drink. He also had a habit of appropriating other people's property, when the opportunity offered of his doing so without being seen. Collar-straps, padlocks, perch-bolts, and things even of greater value belonging to others found their way with remarkable rapidity and in great quantities to Polikey's home. He did not, however, keep such things for his own use, but sold them whenever he could find a purchaser. His payment consisted chiefly of whiskey, though sometimes he received cash.

This sort of employment, as his neighbors said, was both light and profitable; it required neither education nor labor. It had one drawback, however, which was calculated to reconcile his victims to their losses: Though he could for a time have all his needs supplied without expending either labor or money, there was always the possibility of his methods being discovered; and this result was sure to be followed by a long term of imprisonment. This impending danger made life a burden for Polikey and his family.

Such a setback indeed very nearly happened to Polikey early in his career. He married while still young, and God gave him much happiness. His wife, who was a shepherd's daughter, was a strong, intelligent, hard-working woman. She bore him many children, each of whom was said to be better than the preceding one.

Polikey still continued to steal, but once was caught with some small articles belonging to others in his possession. Among them was a pair of leather reins, the property of another peasant, who beat him severely and reported him to his mistress.

From that time on Polikey was an object of suspicion, and he was twice again detected in similar escapades. By this time the people began to abuse him, and the clerk of the court threatened to recruit him into the army as a soldier (which is regarded by the peasants as a great punishment and disgrace). His noble mistress severely reprimanded him; his wife wept from grief for his downfall, and everything went from bad to worse.

Polikey, notwithstanding his weakness, was a good-natured sort of man, but his love of strong drink had so overcome every moral instinct that at times he was scarcely responsible for his actions. This habit he vainly endeavored to overcome. It often happened that when he returned home intoxicated, his wife, losing all patience, roundly cursed him and cruelly beat him. At times he would cry like a child, and bemoan his fate, saying: "Unfortunate man that I am, what shall I do? LET MY EYES BURST INTO PIECES if I do not forever give up the vile habit! I will not again touch vodki."

In spite of all his promises of reform, but a short period (perhaps a month) would elapse when Polikey would again mysteriously disappear from his home and be lost for several days on a spree.

"From what source does he get the money he spends so freely?" the neighbors inquired of each other, as they sadly shook their heads.

One of his most unfortunate exploits in the matter of stealing was in connection with a clock which belonged to the estate of his mistress. The clock stood in the private office of the noblewoman, and was so old as to have outlived its usefulness, and was simply kept as an heirloom. It so happened that Polikey went into the office one day when no one was present but himself, and, seeing the old clock, it seemed to possess a peculiar fascination for him, and he speedily transferred it to his person. He carried it to a town not far from the village, where he very readily found a purchaser.

As if purposely to secure his punishment, it happened that the storekeeper to whom he sold it proved to be a relative of one of the court servants, and who, when he visited his friend on the next holiday, related all about his purchase of the clock.

An investigation was immediately instituted, and all the details of Polikey's transaction were brought to light and reported to his noble mistress. He was called into her presence, and, when confronted with the story of the theft, broke down and confessed all. He fell on his knees before the noblewoman and plead with her for mercy. The kind-hearted lady lectured him about God, the salvation of his soul, and his future life. She talked to him also about the misery and disgrace he brought upon his family, and altogether so worked upon his feelings that he cried like a child. In conclusion his kind mistress said: "I will forgive you this time on the condition that you promise faithfully to reform, and never again to take what does not belong to you."

Polikey, still weeping, replied: "I will never steal again in all my life, and if I break my promise may the earth open and swallow me up, and let my body be burned with red-hot irons!"

Polikey returned to his home, and throwing himself on the oven spent the entire day weeping and repeating the promise made to his mistress.

From that time on he was not again caught stealing, but his life became extremely sad, for he was regarded with suspicion by every one and pointed to as a thief.

When the time came round for securing recruits for the army, all the peasants singled out Polikey as the first to be taken. The superintendent was especially anxious to get rid of him, and went to his mistress to induce her to have him sent away. The kind-hearted and merciful woman, remembering the peasant's repentance, refused to grant the superintendent's request, and told him he must take some other man in his stead.

# CHAPTER II

One evening Polikey was sitting on his bed beside the table, preparing some medicine for the cattle, when suddenly the door was thrown wide open, and Aksiutka, a young girl from the court, rushed in. Almost out of breath, she said: "My mistress has ordered you, Polikey Illitch,[17] to come up to the court at once!"

The girl was standing and still breathing heavily from her late exertion as she continued: "Egor Mikhailovitch, the superintendent, has been to see our lady about having you drafted into the army, and, Polikey Illitch, your name was mentioned among others. Our lady has sent me to tell you to come up to the court immediately."

As soon as Aksiutka had delivered her message she left the room in the same abrupt manner in which she had entered.

---

[17] son of Ilia

Akulina, without saying a word, got up and brought her husband's boots to him. They were poor, worn-out things which some soldier had given him, and his wife did not glance at him as she handed them to him.

"Are you going to change your shirt, Illitch?" she asked, at last.

"No," replied Polikey.

Akulina did not once look at him all the time he was putting on his boots and preparing to go to the court. Perhaps, after all, it was better that she did not do so. His face was very pale and his lips trembled. He slowly combed his hair and was about to depart without saying a word, when his wife stopped him to arrange the ribbon on his shirt, and, after toying a little with his coat, she put his hat on for him and he left the little home.

Polikey's next-door neighbors were a joiner and his wife. A thin partition only separated the two families, and each could hear what the other said and did.

Soon after Polikey's departure a woman was heard to say: "Well, Polikey Illitch, so your mistress has sent for you!"

The voice was that of the joiner's wife on the other side of the partition. Akulina and the woman had quarrelled that morning about some trifling thing done by one of Polikey's children, and it afforded her the greatest pleasure to learn that her neighbor had been summoned into the presence of his noble mistress. She looked upon such a circumstance as a bad omen. She continued talking to herself and said: "Perhaps she wants to send him to the town to make some purchases for her household. I did not suppose she would select such a faithful man as you are to perform such a service for her. If it should prove that she DOES want to send you to the next town, just buy me a quarter-pound of tea. Will you, Polikey Illitch?"

Poor Akulina, on hearing the joiner's wife talking so unkindly of her husband, could hardly suppress the tears, and, the tirade continuing, she at last became angry, and wished she could in some way punish her.

Forgetting her neighbor's unkindness, her thoughts soon turned in another direction, and glancing at her sleeping children she said to herself that they might soon be orphans and she herself a soldier's widow. This thought greatly distressed her, and burying her face in her hands she seated herself on the bed, where several of her progeny were fast asleep. Presently a little voice interrupted her meditations by crying out, "Mamushka,[18] you are crushing me," and the child pulled her nightdress from under her mother's arms.

Akulina, with her head still resting on her hands, said: "Perhaps it would be better if we all should die. I only seem to have brought you into the world to suffer sorrow and misery."

Unable longer to control her grief, she burst into violent weeping, which served to increase the amusement of the joiner's

[18] little mother

wife, who had not forgotten the morning's squabble, and she laughed loudly at her neighbor's woe.

# CHAPTER III

About half an hour had passed when the youngest child began to cry and Akulina arose to feed it. She had by this time ceased to weep, and after feeding the infant she again fell into her old position, with her face buried in her hands. She was very pale, but this only increased her beauty. After a time she raised her head, and staring at the burning candle she began to question herself as to why she had married, and as to the reason that the Czar required so many soldiers.

Presently she heard steps outside, and knew that her husband was returning. She hurriedly wiped away the last traces of her tears as she arose to let him pass into the centre of the room.

Polikey made his appearance with a look of triumph on his face, threw his hat on the bed, and hastily removed his coat; but not a word did he utter.

Akulina, unable to restrain her impatience, asked, "Well, what did she want with you?"

"Pshaw!" he replied, "it is very well known that Polikushka is considered the worst man in the village; but when it comes to business of importance, who is selected then? Why, Polikushka, of course."

"What kind of business?" Akulina timidly inquired.

But Polikey was in no hurry to answer her question. He lighted his pipe with a very imposing air, and spit several times on the floor before he replied.

Still retaining his pompous manner, he said, "She has ordered me to go to a certain merchant in the town and collect a considerable sum of money."

"You to collect money?" questioned Akulina.

Polikey only shook his head and smiled significantly, saying:

"'You,' the mistress said to me, 'are a man resting under a grave suspicion – a man who is considered unsafe to trust in any capacity; but I have faith in you, and will intrust you with this important business of mine in preference to any one else.'"

Polikey related all this in a loud voice, so that his neighbor might hear what he had to say.

"'You promised me to reform,' my noble mistress said to me, 'and I will be the first to show you how much faith I have in your promise. I want you to ride into town, and, going to the principal merchant there, collect a sum of money from him and bring it to me.' I said to my mistress: 'Everything you order shall be done. I will only too gladly obey your slightest wish.'

"Then my mistress said: 'Do you understand, Polikey, that your future lot depends upon the faithful performance of this duty I impose upon you?' I replied: 'Yes, I understand everything, and feel that I will succeed in performing acceptably any task which you may impose upon me. I have been accused of every kind of evil deed that it is possible to charge a man with, but I have never done anything seriously wrong against you, your honor.' In this way I talked to our mistress until I succeeded in convincing her that my repentance was sincere, and she became greatly softened toward me, saying, 'If you are successful I will give you the first place at the court.'"

"And how much money are you to collect?" inquired Akulina.

"Fifteen hundred rubles," carelessly answered Polikey.

Akulina sadly shook her head as she asked, "When are you to start?"

"She ordered me to leave here to-morrow," Polikey replied. "'Take any horse you please,' she said. 'Come to the office, and I will see you there and wish you God-speed on your journey.'"

"Glory to Thee, O Lord!" said Akulina, as she arose and made the sign of the cross. "God, I am sure, will bless you, Illitch," she added, in a whisper, so that the people on the other side of the partition could not hear what she said, all the while holding on to his sleeve. "Illitch," she cried at last, excitedly, "for God's sake promise me that you will not touch a drop of vodki. Take an oath before God, and kiss the cross, so that I may be sure that you will not break your promise!"

Polikey replied in most contemptuous tones: "Do you think I will dare to touch vodki when I shall have such a large sum of money in my care?"

"Akulina, have a clean shirt ready for the morning," were his parting words for the night.

So Polikey and his wife went to sleep in a happy frame of mind and full of bright dreams for the future.

# CHAPTER IV

Very early the next morning, almost before the stars had hidden themselves from view, there was seen standing before Polikey's home a low wagon, the same in which the superintendent himself used to ride; and harnessed to it was a large-boned, dark-brown mare, called for some unknown reason by the name of Baraban (drum). Aniutka, Polikey's eldest daughter, in spite of the heavy rain and the cold wind which was blowing, stood outside barefooted and held (not without some fear) the reins in ore hand, while with the other she endeavored to keep her green and yellow overcoat wound around her body, and also to hold Polikey's sheepskin coat.

In the house there were the greatest noise and confusion. The morning was still so dark that the little daylight there was failed to penetrate through the broken panes of glass, the window being stuffed in many places with rags and paper to exclude the cold air.

Akulina ceased from her cooking for a while and helped to get Polikey ready for the journey. Most of the children were still in bed, very likely as a protection against the cold, for Akulina had taken away the big overcoat which usually covered them and had substituted a shawl of her own. Polikey's shirt was all ready, nice and clean, but his shoes badly needed repairing, and this fact caused his devoted wife much anxiety. She took from her own feet the thick woollen stockings she was wearing, and gave them to Polikey. She then began to repair his shoes, patching up the holes so as to protect his feet from dampness.

While this was going on he was sitting on the side of the bed with his feet dangling over the edge, and trying to turn the sash which confined his coat at the waist. He was anxious to look as clean as possible, and he declared his sash looked like a dirty rope.

One of his daughters, enveloped in a sheepskin coat, was sent to a neighbor's house to borrow a hat.

Within Polikey's home the greatest confusion reigned, for the court servants were constantly arriving with innumerable small orders which they wished Polikey to execute for them in town. One wanted needles, another tea, another tobacco, and last came the joiner's wife, who by this time had prepared her samovar, and, anxious to make up the quarrel of the previous day, brought the traveller a cup of tea.

Neighbor Nikita refused the loan of the hat, so the old one had to be patched up for the occasion. This occupied some time, as there were many holes in it.

Finally Polikey was all ready, and jumping on the wagon started on his journey, after first making the sign of the cross.

At the last moment his little boy, Mishka, ran to the door, begging to be given a short ride; and then his little daughter, Mashka, appeared on the scene and pleaded that she, too, might have a ride, declaring that she would be quite warm enough without furs.

Polikey stopped the horse on hearing the children, and Akulina placed them in the wagon, together with two others belonging to a neighbor – all anxious to have a short ride.

As Akulina helped the little ones into the wagon she took occasion to remind Polikey of the solemn promise he had made her not to touch a drop of vodki during the journey.

Polikey drove the children as far as the blacksmith's place, where he let them out of the wagon, telling them they must return home. He then arranged his clothing, and, setting his hat firmly on his head, started his horse on a trot.

The two children, Mishka and Mashka, both barefooted, started running at such a rapid pace that a strange dog from another village, seeing them flying over the road, dropped his tail between his legs and ran home squealing.

The weather was very cold, a sharp cutting wind blowing continuously; but this did not disturb Polikey, whose mind was engrossed with pleasant thoughts. As he rode through the wintry blasts he kept repeating to himself: "So I am the man they wanted to send to Siberia, and whom they threatened to enroll as a soldier – the same man whom every one abused, and said he was lazy, and who was pointed out as a thief and given the meanest work on the estate to do! Now I am going to receive a large sum of money, for which my mistress is sending me because she trusts me. I am also riding in the same wagon that the superintendent himself uses when he is riding as a representative of the court. I have the same harness, leather horse-collar, reins, and all the other gear."

Polikey, filled with pride at thought of the mission with which he had been intrusted, drew himself up with an air of pride, and, fixing his old hat more firmly on his head, buttoned his coat tightly about him and urged his horse to greater speed.

"Just to think," he continued; "I shall have in my possession three thousand half-rubles,[19] and will carry them in my bosom. If I wished to I might run away to Odessa instead of taking the money to my mistress. But no; I will not do that. I will surely carry the money straight to the one who has been kind enough to trust me."

When Polikey reached the first kabak (tavern) he found that from long habit the mare was naturally turning her head toward it; but he would not allow her to stop, though money had been given him to purchase both food and drink. Striking the animal a sharp blow with the whip, he passed by the tavern. The performance was repeated when he reached the next kabak, which looked very inviting; but he resolutely set his face against entering, and passed on.

---

[19] the peasant manner of speaking of money so as to make it appear a larger sum than it really is

About noon he arrived at his destination, and getting down from the wagon approached the gate of the merchant's house where the servants of the court always stopped. Opening it he led the mare through, and (after unharnessing her) fed her. This done, he next entered the house and had dinner with the merchant's workingman, and to them he related what an important mission he had been sent on, making himself very amusing by the pompous air which he assumed. Dinner over, he carried a letter to the merchant which the noblewoman had given him to deliver.

The merchant, knowing thoroughly the reputation which Polikey bore, felt doubtful of trusting him with so much money, and somewhat anxiously inquired if he really had received orders to carry so many rubles.

Polikey tried to appear offended at this question, but did not succeed, and he only smiled.

The merchant, after reading the letter a second time and being convinced that all was right, gave Polikey the money, which he put in his bosom for safe-keeping.

On his way to the house he did not once stop at any of the shops he passed. The clothing establishments possessed no attractions for him, and after he had safely passed them all he stood for a moment, feeling very pleased that he had been able to withstand temptation, and then went on his way.

"I have money enough to buy up everything," he said; "but I will not do so."

The numerous commissions which he had received compelled him to go to the bazaar. There he bought only what had been ordered, but he could not resist the temptation to ask the price of a very handsome sheep-skin coat which attracted his attention. The merchant to whom he spoke looked at Polikey and smiled, not believing that he had sufficient money to purchase such an expensive coat. But

Polikey, pointing to his breast, said that he could buy out the whole shop if he wished to. He thereupon ordered the shop-keeper to take his measure. He tried the coat on and looked himself over carefully, testing the quality and blowing upon the hair to see that none of it came out. Finally, heaving a deep sigh, he took it off.

"The price is too high," he said. "If you could let me have it for fifteen rubles—"

But the merchant cut him short by snatching the coat from him and throwing it angrily to one side.

Polikey left the bazaar and returned to the merchant's house in high spirits.

After supper he went out and fed the mare, and prepared everything for the night. Returning to the house he got up on the stove to rest, and while there he took out the envelope which contained the money and looked long and earnestly at it. He could not read, but asked one of those present to tell him what the writing on the envelope meant. It was simply the address and the announcement that it contained fifteen hundred rubles.

The envelope was made of common paper and was sealed with dark-brown sealing wax. There was one large seal in the centre and four smaller ones at the corners. Polikey continued to examine it carefully, even inserting his finger till he touched the crisp notes. He appeared to take a childish delight in having so much money in his possession.

Having finished his examination, he put the envelope inside the lining of his old battered hat, and placing both under his head he went to sleep; but during the night he frequently awoke and always felt to know if the money was safe. Each time that he found that it was safe he rejoiced at the thought that he, Polikey, abused and regarded by every one as a thief, was intrusted with the care of such a large sum of money, and also that he was about to return with it quite as safely as the superintendent himself could have done.

# CHAPTER V

Before dawn the next morning Polikey was up, and after harnessing the mare and looking in his hat to see that the money was all right, he started on his return journey.

Many times on the way Polikey took off his hat to see that the money was safe. Once he said to himself, "I think that perhaps it would be better if I should put it in my bosom." This would necessitate the untying of his sash, so he decided to keep it still in his hat, or until he should have made half the journey, when he would be compelled to stop to feed his horse and to rest.

He said to himself: "The lining is not sewn in very strongly and the envelope might fall out, so I think I had better not take off my hat until I reach home."

The money was safe – at least, so it seemed to him – and he began to think how grateful his mistress would be to him, and in his excited imagination he saw the five rubles he was so sure of receiving.

Once more he examined the hat to see that the money was safe, and finding everything all right he put on his hat and pulled it well down over his ears, smiling all the while at his own thoughts.

Akulina had carefully sewed all the holes in the hat, but it burst out in other places owing to Polikey's removing it so often.

In the darkness he did not notice the new rents, and tried to push the envelope further under the lining, and in doing so pushed one corner of it through the plush.

The sun was getting high in the heavens, and Polikey having slept but little the previous night and feeling its warm rays fell fast asleep, after first pressing his hat more firmly on his head. By this action he forced the envelope still further through the plush, and as he rode along his head bobbed up and down.

Polikey did not awake till he arrived near his own house, and his first act was to put his hand to his head to learn if his hat was all right. Finding that it was in its place, he did not think it necessary to examine it and see that the money was safe. Touching the mare gently with the whip she started into a trot, and as he rode along he arranged in his own mind how much he was to receive. With the air of a man already holding a high position at the court, he looked around him with an expression of lofty scorn on his face.

As he neared his house he could see before him the one room which constituted their humble home, and the joiner's wife next door carrying her rolls of linen. He saw also the office of the court and his mistress's house, where he hoped he would be able presently to prove that he was an honest, trustworthy man.

He reasoned with himself that any person can be abused by lying tongues, but when his mistress would see him she would say: "Well done, Polikey; you have shown that you can be honest. Here are three –

it may be five – perhaps ten – rubles for you;" and also she would order tea for him, and might treat him to vodki – who knows?

The latter thought gave him great pleasure, as he was feeling very cold.

Speaking aloud he said: "What a happy holy-day we can have with ten rubles! Having so much money, I could pay Nikita the four rubles fifty kopecks which I owe him, and yet have some left to buy shoes for the children."

When near the house Polikey began to arrange his clothes, smoothing down his fur collar, re-tying his sash, and stroking his hair. To do the latter he had to take off his hat, and when doing so felt in the lining for the envelope. Quicker and quicker he ran his hand around the lining, and not finding the money used both hands, first one and then the other. But the envelope was not to be found.

Polikey was by this time greatly distressed, and his face was white with fear as he passed his hand through the crown of his old hat. Polikey stopped the mare and began a diligent search through the wagon and its contents. Not finding the precious envelope, he felt in all his pockets – BUT THE MONEY COULD NOT BE FOUND!

Wildly clutching at his hair, he exclaimed: "Batiushka! What will I do now? What will become of me?" At the same time he realized that he was near his neighbors' house and could be seen by them; so he turned the mare around, and, pulling his hat down securely upon his head, he rode quickly back in search of his lost treasure.

# CHAPTER VI

The whole day passed without any one in the village of Pokrovski having seen anything of Polikey. During the afternoon his mistress inquired many times as to his whereabouts, and sent Aksiutka frequently to Akulina, who each time sent back word that Polikey had not yet returned, saying also that perhaps the merchant had kept him, or that something had happened to the mare.

His poor wife felt a heavy load upon her heart, and was scarcely able to do her housework and put everything in order for the next day (which was to be a holy-day). The children also anxiously awaited their father's appearance, and, though for different reasons, could hardly restrain their impatience. The noblewoman and Akulina were concerned only in regard to Polikey himself, while the children were interested most in what he would bring them from the town.

The only news received by the villagers during the day concerning Polikey was to the effect that neighboring peasants had seen him running up and down the road and asking every one he met if he or she had found an envelope.

One of them had seen him also walking by the side of his tired-out horse. "I thought," said he, "that the man was drunk, and had not fed his horse for two days – the animal looked so exhausted."

Unable to sleep, and with her heart palpitating at every sound, Akulina lay awake all night vainly awaiting Polikey's return. When the cock crowed the third time she was obliged to get up to attend to the fire. Day was just dawning and the church-bells had begun to ring. Soon all the children were also up, but there was still no tidings of the missing husband and father.

In the morning the chill blasts of winter entered their humble home, and on looking out they saw that the houses, fields, and roads were thickly covered with snow. The day was clear and cold, as if befitting the holy-day they were about to celebrate. They were able to see a long distance from the house, but no one was in sight.

Akulina was busy baking cakes, and had it not been for the joyous shouts of the children she would not have known that Polikey was coming up the road, for a few minutes later he came in with a bundle in his hand and walked quietly to his corner. Akulina noticed that he was very pale and that his face bore an expression of suffering – as if he would like to have cried but could not do so. But she did not stop to study it, but excitedly inquired: "What! Illitch, is everything all right with you?"

He slowly muttered something, but his wife could not understand what he said.

"What!" she cried out, "have you been to see our mistress?"

Polikey still sat on the bed in his corner, glaring wildly about him, and smiling bitterly. He did not reply for a long time, and Akulina again cried:

"Eh? Illitch! Why don't you answer me? Why don't you speak?"

Finally he said: "Akulina, I delivered the money to our mistress; and oh, how she thanked me!" Then he suddenly looked about him, with an anxious, startled air, and with a sad smile on his lips. Two things in the room seemed to engross the most of his attention: the baby in the cradle, and the rope which was attached to the ladder. Approaching the cradle, he began with his thin fingers quickly to untie the knot in the rope by which the two were connected. After untying it he stood for a few moments looking silently at the baby.

Akulina did not notice this proceeding, and with her cakes on the board went to place them in a corner.

Polikey quickly hid the rope beneath his coat, and again seated himself on the bed.

"What is it that troubles you, Illitch?" inquired Akulina. "You are not yourself."

"I have not slept," he answered.

Suddenly a dark shadow crossed the window, and a minute later the girl Aksiutka quickly entered the room, exclaiming:

"The boyarinia commands you, Polikey Illitch, to come to her this moment!"

Polikey looked first at Akulina and then at the girl.

"This moment!" he cried. "What more is wanted?"

He spoke the last sentence so softly that Akulina became quieted in her mind, thinking that perhaps their mistress intended to reward her husband.

"Say that I will come immediately," he said.

But Polikey failed to follow the girl, and went instead to another place.

From the porch of his house there was a ladder reaching to the attic. Arriving at the foot of the ladder Polikey looked around him, and seeing no one about, he quickly ascended to the garret.

*** 

Meanwhile the girl had reached her mistress's house.

"What does it mean that Polikey does not come?" said the noblewoman impatiently. "Where can he be? Why does he not come at once?"

Aksiutka flew again to his house and demanded to see Polikey.

"He went a long time ago," answered Akulina, and looking around with an expression of fear on her face, she added, "He may have fallen asleep somewhere on the way."

About this time the joiner's wife, with hair unkempt and clothes bedraggled, went up to the loft to gather the linen which she had previously put there to dry. Suddenly a cry of horror was heard, and the woman, with her eyes closed, and crazed by fear, ran down the ladder like a cat.

"Illitch," she cried, "has hanged himself!"

Poor Akulina ran up the ladder before any of the people, who had gathered from the surrounding houses, could prevent her. With a loud shriek she fell back as if dead, and would surely have been killed had not one of the spectators succeeded in catching her in his arms.

Before dark the same day a peasant of the village, while returning from the town, found the envelope containing Polikey's money on the roadside, and soon after delivered it to the boyarinia.

# Story 5

## THE CANDLE.

***

"Ye have heard that it hath been said, an
eye for an eye and a tooth for a tooth:
but I say unto you,
That ye resist not evil."
– ST. MATTHEW

It was in the time of serfdom – many
years before Alexander II.'s liberation of
the sixty million serfs in 1862. In those
days the people were ruled by different
kinds of lords. There were not a few who,
remembering God, treated their slaves in
a humane manner, and not as beasts of
burden, while there were others who were
seldom known to perform a kind or generous action; but the most barbarous and
tyrannical of all were those former serfs
who arose from the dirt and became
princes.

It was this latter class who made life literally a burden to those who were unfortunate enough to come under their rule. Many of them had arisen from the ranks of the peasantry to become superintendents of noblemen's estates.

The peasants were obliged to work for their master a certain number of days each week. There was plenty of land and water and the soil was rich and fertile, while the meadows and forests were sufficient to supply the needs of both the peasants and their lord.

There was a certain nobleman who had chosen a superintendent from the peasantry on one of his other estates. No sooner had the power to govern been vested in this newly-made official than he began to practice the most outrageous cruelties upon the poor serfs who had been placed under his control. Although this man had a wife and two married daughters, and was making so much money that he could have lived happily without transgressing in any way against either God or man, yet he was filled with envy and jealousy and deeply sunk in sin.

Michael Simeonovitch began his persecutions by compelling the peasants to perform more days of service on the estate every week than the laws obliged them to work. He established a brick-yard, in which he forced the men and women to do excessive labor, selling the bricks for his own profit.

On one occasion the overworked serfs sent a delegation to Moscow to complain of their treatment to their lord, but they obtained no satisfaction. When the poor peasants returned disconsolate from the nobleman their superintendent determined to have revenge for their boldness in going above him for redress, and their life and that of their fellow-victims became worse than before.

It happened that among the serfs there were some very treacherous people who would falsely accuse their fellows of wrong-doing and sow seeds of discord among the peasantry, whereupon Michael would become greatly enraged, while his poor subjects began to live in fear of their lives. When the superintendent passed through the village the people would run and hide themselves as from a wild beast. Seeing thus the terror which he had struck to the hearts of the moujiks, Michael's treatment of them became still more vindictive, so that from over-work and ill-usage the lot of the poor serfs was indeed a hard one.

There was a time when it was possible for the peasants, when driven to despair, to devise means whereby they could rid themselves of an inhuman monster such as Simeonovitch, and so these unfortunate people began to consider whether something could not be done to relieve THEM of their intolerable yoke. They would hold little meetings in secret places to bewail their misery and to confer with one another as to which would be the best way to act. Now and then the boldest of the gathering would rise and address his companions in this strain: "How much longer can we tolerate such a villain to rule over us? Let us make an end of it at once, for it were better for us to perish than to suffer. It is surely not a sin to kill such a devil in human form."

It happened once, before the Easter holidays, that one of these meetings was held in the woods, where Michael had sent the serfs to make a clearance for their master. At noon they assembled to eat their dinner and to hold a consultation. "Why can't we leave now?" said one. "Very soon we shall be reduced to nothing. Already we are almost worked to death – there being no rest, night or day, either for us or our poor women. If anything should be done in a way not exactly to please him he will find fault and perhaps flog some of us to death – as was the case with poor Simeon, whom he killed not long ago. Only recently Anisim was tortured in irons till he died. We certainly cannot stand this much longer." "Yes," said another, "what is the use of waiting? Let us act at once. Michael will be here this evening, and will be certain to abuse us shamefully. Let us, then, thrust him from his horse and with one blow of an axe give him what he deserves, and thus end our misery. We can then dig a big hole and bury him like a dog, and no one will know what became of him. Now let us come to an agreement – to stand together as one man and not to betray one another."

The last speaker was Vasili Minayeff, who, if possible, had more cause to complain of Michael's cruelty than any of his fellow-serfs. The superintendent was in the habit of flogging him severely every week, and he took also Vasili's wife to serve him as cook.

Accordingly, during the evening that followed this meeting in the woods Michael arrived on the scene on horseback. He began at once to find fault with the manner in which the work had been done, and to complain because some lime-trees had been cut down.

"I told you not to cut down any lime-trees!" shouted the enraged superintendent. "Who did this thing? Tell me at once, or I shall flog every one of you!"

On investigation, a peasant named Sidor was pointed out as the guilty one, and his face was roundly slapped. Michael also severely punished Vasili, because he had not done sufficient work, after which the master rode safely home.

In the evening the serfs again assembled, and poor Vasili said: "Oh, what kind of people ARE we, anyway? We are only sparrows, and not men at all! We agree to stand by each other, but as soon as the time for action comes we all run and hide. Once a lot of sparrows conspired against a hawk, but no sooner did the bird of prey appear than they sneaked off in the grass. Selecting one of the choicest sparrows, the hawk took it away to eat, after which the others came out crying, 'Twee-twee!' and found that one was missing. 'Who is killed?' they asked. 'Vanka! Well, he deserved it.' You, my friends, are acting in just the same manner. When Michael attacked Sidor you should have stood by your promise. Why didn't you arise, and with one stroke put an end to him and to our misery?"

The effect of this speech was to make the peasants more firm in their determination to kill their superintendent. The latter had already given orders that they should be ready to plough during the Easter holidays, and to sow the field with oats, whereupon the serfs became stricken with grief, and gathered in Vasili's house to hold another indignation meeting. "If he has really forgotten God," they said, "and shall continue to commit such crimes against us, it is truly necessary that we should kill him. If not, let us perish, for it can make no difference to us now."

This despairing programme, however, met with considerable opposition from a peaceably-inclined man named Peter Mikhayeff. "Brethren," said he, "you are contemplating a grievous sin. The taking of human life is a very serious matter. Of course it is easy to end the mortal existence of a man, but what will become of the souls of those who commit the deed? If Michael continues to act toward us unjustly God will surely punish him. But, my friends, we must have patience."

This pacific utterance only served to intensify the anger of Vasili. Said he: "Peter is forever repeating the same old story, 'It is a sin to kill any one.' Certainly it is sinful to murder; but we should consider the kind of man we are dealing with. We all know it is wrong to kill a good man, but even God would take away the life of such a dog as he is. It is our duty, if we have any love for mankind, to shoot a dog that is mad. It is a sin to let him live. If, therefore, we are to suffer at all, let it be in the interests of the people – and they will thank us for it. If we remain quiet any longer a flogging will be our only reward. You are talking nonsense, Mikhayeff. Why don't you think of the sin we shall be committing if we work during the Easter holidays – for you will refuse to work then yourself?"

"Well, then," replied Peter, "if they shall send me to plough, I will go. But I shall not be going of my own free will, and God will know whose sin it is, and shall punish the offender accordingly. Yet we must not forget him. Brethren, I am not giving you my own views only. The law of God is not to return evil for evil; indeed, if you try in this way to stamp out wickedness it will come upon you all the stronger. It is not difficult for you to kill the man, but his blood will surely stain your own soul. You may think you have killed a bad man – that you have gotten rid of evil – but you will soon find out that the seeds of still greater wickedness have been planted within you. If you yield to misfortune it will surely come to you."

As Peter was not without sympathizers among the peasants, the poor serfs were consequently divided into two groups: the followers of Vasili and those who held the views of Mikhayeff.

On Easter Sunday no work was done. Toward the evening an elder came to the peasants from the nobleman's court and said: "Our superintendent, Michael Simeonovitch, orders you to go to-morrow to plough the field for the oats." Thus the official went through the village and directed the men to prepare for work the next day – some by the river and others by the roadway. The poor people were almost overcome with grief, many of them shedding tears, but none dared to disobey the orders of their master.

On the morning of Easter Monday, while the church bells were calling the inhabitants to religious services, and while every one else was about to enjoy a holiday, the unfortunate serfs started for the field to plough. Michael arose rather late and took a walk about the farm. The domestic servants were through with their work and had dressed themselves for the day, while Michael's wife and their widowed daughter (who was visiting them, as was her custom on holidays) had been to church and returned. A steaming samovar awaited them, and they began to drink tea with Michael, who, after lighting his pipe, called the elder to him.

"Well," said the superintendent, "have you ordered the moujiks to plough to-day?"

"Yes, sir, I did," was the reply.

"Have they all gone to the field?"

"Yes, sir; all of them. I directed them myself where to begin."

"That is all very well. You gave the orders, but are they ploughing? Go at once and see, and you may tell them that I shall be there after dinner. I shall expect to find one and a half acres done for every two ploughs, and the work must be well done; otherwise they shall be severely punished, notwithstanding the holiday."

"I hear, sir, and obey."

The elder started to go, but Michael called him back. After hesitating for some time, as if he felt very uneasy, he said:

"By the way, listen to what those scoundrels say about me. Doubtless some of them will curse me, and I want you to report the exact words. I know what villains they are. They don't find work at all pleasant. They would rather lie down all day and do nothing. They would like to eat and drink and make merry on holidays, but they forget that if the ploughing is not done it will soon be too late. So you go and listen to what is said, and tell it to me in detail. Go at once."

"I hear, sir, and obey."

Turning his back and mounting his horse, the elder was soon at the field where the serfs were hard at work.

It happened that Michael's wife, a very good-hearted woman, overheard the conversation which her husband had just been holding with the elder. Approaching him, she said:

"My good friend, Mishinka,[20] I beg of you to consider the importance and solemnity of this holy-day. Do not sin, for Christ's sake. Let the poor moujiks go home."

---

[20] diminutive of Michael

Michael laughed, but made no reply to his wife's humane request. Finally he said to her:

"You've not been whipped for a very long time, and now you have become bold enough to interfere in affairs that are not your own."

"Mishinka," she persisted, "I have had a frightful dream concerning you. You had better let the moujiks go."

"Yes," said he; "I perceive that you have gained so much flesh of late that you think you would not feel the whip. Lookout!"

Rudely thrusting his hot pipe against her cheek, Michael chased his wife from the room, after which he ordered his dinner. After eating a hearty meal consisting of cabbage-soup, roast pig, meat-cake, pastry with milk, jelly, sweet cakes, and vodki, he called his woman cook to him and ordered her to be seated and sing songs, Simeonovitch accompanying her on the guitar.

While the superintendent was thus enjoying himself to the fullest satisfaction in the musical society of his cook the elder returned, and, making a low bow to his superior, proceeded to give the desired information concerning the serfs.

"Well," asked Michael, "did they plough?"

"Yes," replied the elder; "they have accomplished about half the field."

"Is there no fault to be found?"

"Not that I could discover. The work seems to be well done. They are evidently afraid of you."

"How is the soil?"

"Very good. It appears to be quite soft."

"Well," said Simeonovitch, after a pause, "what did they say about me? Cursed me, I suppose?"

As the elder hesitated somewhat, Michael commanded him to speak and tell him the whole truth. "Tell me all," said he; "I want to know their exact words. If you tell me the truth I shall reward you; but if you conceal anything from me you will be punished. See here, Catherine, pour out a glass of vodki to give him courage!"

After drinking to the health of his superior, the elder said to himself: "It is not my fault if they do not praise him. I shall tell him the truth." Then turning suddenly to the superintendent he said:

"They complain, Michael Simeonovitch! They complain bitterly."

"But what did they say?" demanded Michael. "Tell me!"

"Well, one thing they said was, 'He does not believe in God.'"

Michael laughed. "Who said that?" he asked.

"It seemed to be their unanimous opinion. 'He has been overcome by the Evil One,' they said."

"Very good," laughed the superintendent; "but tell me what each of them said. What did Vasili say?"

The elder did not wish to betray his people, but he had a certain grudge against Vasili, and he said:

"He cursed you more than did any of the others."

"But what did he say?"

"It is awful to repeat it, sir. Vasili said, 'He shall die like a dog, having no chance to repent!'"

"Oh, the villain!" exclaimed Michael. "He would kill me if he were not afraid. All right, Vasili; we shall have an accounting with you. And Tishka – he called me a dog, I suppose?"

"Well," said the elder, "they all spoke of you in anything but complimentary terms; but it is mean in me to repeat what they said."

"Mean or not you must tell me, I say!"

"Some of them declared that your back should be broken."

Simeonovitch appeared to enjoy this immensely, for he laughed outright. "We shall see whose back will be the first to be broken," said he. "Was that Tishka's opinion? While I did not suppose they would say anything good about me, I did not expect such curses and threats. And Peter Mikhayeff – was that fool cursing me too?"

"No; he did not curse you at all. He appeared to be the only silent one among them. Mikhayeff is a very wise moujik, and he surprises me very much. At his actions all the other peasants seemed amazed."

"What did he do?"

"He did something remarkable. He was diligently ploughing, and as I approached him I heard some one singing very sweetly. Looking between the ploughshares, I observed a bright object shining."

"Well, what was it? Hurry up!"

"It was a small, five-kopeck wax candle, burning brightly, and the wind was unable to blow it out. Peter, wearing a new shirt, sang beautiful hymns as he ploughed, and no matter how he handled the implement the candle continued to burn. In my presence he fixed the plough, shaking it violently, but the bright little object between the colters remained undisturbed."

"And what did Mikhayeff say?"

"He said nothing – except when, on seeing me, he gave me the holy-day salutation, after which he went on his way singing and ploughing as before. I did not say anything to him, but, on approaching the other moujiks, I found that they were laughing and making sport of their silent companion. 'It is a great sin to plough on Easter Monday,' they said. 'You could not get absolution from your sin if you were to pray all your life.'"

"And did Mikhayeff make no reply?"

"He stood long enough to say: 'There should be peace on earth and good-will to men,' after which he resumed his ploughing and singing, the candle burning even more brightly than before."

Simeonovitch had now ceased to ridicule, and, putting aside his guitar, his head dropped on his breast and he became lost in thought. Presently he ordered the elder and cook to depart, after which Michael went behind a screen and threw himself upon the bed. He was sighing and moaning, as if in great distress, when his wife came in and spoke kindly to him. He refused to listen to her, exclaiming:

"He has conquered me, and my end is near!"

"Mishinka," said the woman, "arise and go to the moujiks in the field. Let them go home, and everything will be all right. Heretofore you have run far greater risks without any fear, but now you appear to be very much alarmed."

"He has conquered me!" he repeated. "I am lost!"

"What do you mean?" demanded his wife, angrily. "If you will go and do as I tell you there will be no danger. Come, Mishinka," she added, tenderly; "I shall have the saddle-horse brought for you at once."

When the horse arrived the woman persuaded her husband to mount the animal, and to fulfil her request concerning the serfs. When he reached the village a woman opened the gate for him to enter, and as he did so the inhabitants, seeing the brutal superintendent whom everybody feared, ran to hide themselves in their houses, gardens, and other secluded places.

At length Michael reached the other gate, which he found closed also, and, being unable to open it himself while seated on his horse, he called loudly for assistance. As no one responded to his shouts he dismounted and opened the gate, but as he was about to remount, and had one foot in the stirrup, the horse became frightened at some pigs and sprang suddenly to one side. The superintendent fell across the fence and a very sharp picket pierced his stomach, when Michael fell unconscious to the ground.

Toward the evening, when the serfs arrived at the village gate, their horses refused to enter. On looking around, the peasants discovered the dead body of their superintendent lying face downward in a pool of blood, where he had fallen from the fence. Peter Mikhayeff alone had sufficient courage to dismount and approach the prostrate form, his companions riding around the village and entering by way of the back yards. Peter closed the dead man's eyes, after which he put the body in a wagon and took it home.

When the nobleman learned of the fatal accident which had befallen his superintendent, and of the brutal treatment which he had meted out to those under him, he freed the serfs, exacting a small rent for the use of his land and the other agricultural opportunities.

And thus the peasants clearly understood that the power of God is manifested not in evil, but in goodness.

www.ReadHowYouWant.com

You can buy our **Large Type** and **EasyRead** books from our www.ReadHowYouWant.com website, from websites like Amazon.com and through your UK and North American bookshop.

**EasyRead** books are designed to make your reading easy and enjoyable. **EasyRead** books are published in different font sizes, so you can select the font size best for you.

**EasyRead** is for people with normal eyesight who want books in an easy-to-read format.

**EasyRead Comfort** is for people who find reading small print tiring but do not need large print.

**EasyRead Large** is for people who find it easier to read larger print.

The **EasyRead** font, character, word and line spacing have all been set to make it as easy as possible both to recognize a word, and to run your eye along a line of text without losing your place. We split as few words as possible at line ends, as split words make reading harder and can be annoying. For out-of-copyright books, words have been changed to modern spelling (where the sense is not affected), and the original hyphenation of compound words has been retained where this improves word recognition or sense.

With most things you buy, you get a choice, and you can choose the make and model that suits best. There is a big exception – books. You don't get to choose a format that is easy for you to read – you have to read the format the publisher selects.

This "**One Size Fits All**" paradigm **no longer** need apply to books.

At www.ReadHowYouWant.com, you can order a book just as you want it, so you can read it easily. You can choose nearly any format, and at a surprisingly low cost, because of a technical breakthrough that allows us to typeset an individual book automatically, print and bind the book and have it quickly sent directly to you.

You can have your book in **Talking Book** formats (**DAISY or MP3**) or as an **E-book** or in **Braille**.

We have developed totally new visual formats which we hope will help people with **dyslexia** and other print reading disabilities. Look at www.ReadHowYouWant.com for more information.

**Good news for publishers and authors.** There is a big market for large type, personalized and accessible format books. We can help publishers and authors find new market opportunities for their books, and selling your book through www.ReadHowYouWant.com is easy – we do the work for you. Contact us on info@ReadHowYouWant.com.

754667

Printed in Great Britain by
Amazon.co.uk, Ltd.,
Marston Gate.